Praise for Book #1 of the
True Game Series:

"At this point in time, I tend to blanch when, as in Sheri Tepper's *King's Blood Four*, something called a Gamesmaster turns up in the second paragraph. . . . However, in this case I bring this up only to encourage perseverance for readers who may have the same reaction; Tepper transcends her gamesmanship to create a solid fantasy world. . . .

"One particular scene must be mentioned, at the risk of spoiling the surprise at the absolute outrageousness of it all. Perhaps one can be oblique . . . this is certainly the first fantasy novel in which a character appears and *knits* two others into existence (and I really mean knits, as with needles and knit one, purl two). Any author that can carry *that* off has got to have a future."

—Baird Searles
Isaac Asimov's SF Magazine

Other fantasy titles available from
Ace Science Fiction and Fantasy:

The Malacia Tapestry, *Brian Aldiss*
The Face in the Frost, *John Bellairs*
The Phoenix and the Mirror, *Avram Davidson*
The King in Yellow, *Robert W. Chambers*
The Borribles Go for Broke, *Michael de Larrabeiti*
A Lost Tale, *Dale Estey*
The Broken Citadel, *Joyce Ballou Gregorian*
Songs From the Drowned Lands, *Eileen Kernaghan*
The "Fafhrd and Gray Mouser" Series, *Fritz Leiber*
The Door in the Hedge, *Robin McKinley*
Jirel of Joiry, *C.L. Moore*
The "Witch World" Series, *Andre Norton*
The Tomoe Gozen Saga, *Jessica Amanda Salmonson*
King's Blood Four, *Sheri S. Tepper*
The Devil in a Forest, *Gene Wolfe*
Daughter of Witches, *Patricia C. Wrede*
Changeling, *Roger Zelazny*

and much more!

NECROMANCER NINE

SHERI S. TEPPER

ACE FANTASY BOOKS
NEW YORK

NECROMANCER NINE

An Ace Fantasy Book published by arrangement with the
author and her agent, Gloria Safier

PRINTING HISTORY
Ace Original/September 1983

ISBN: 0-441-56853-X

Ace Fantasy Books are published by The Berkley Publishing Group,
200 Madison Avenue, New York, New York 10016
PRINTED IN THE UNITED STATES OF AMERICA

THE ORDER OF DESCENT BY LINEAGE

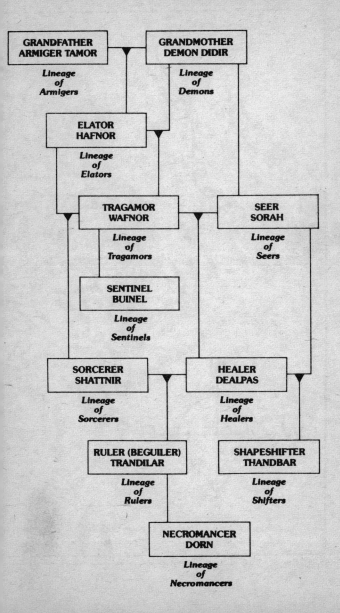

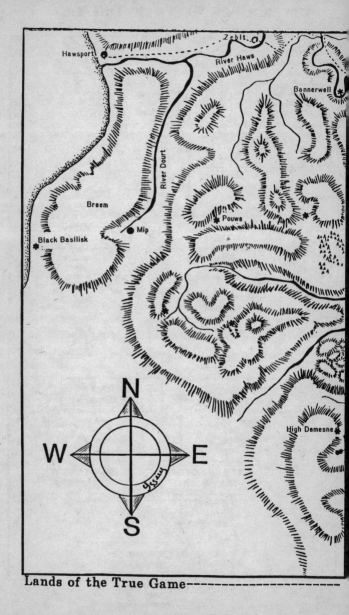

Lands of the True Game————————

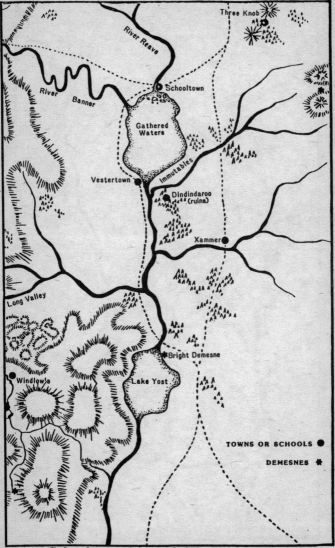

From Schooltown South & West

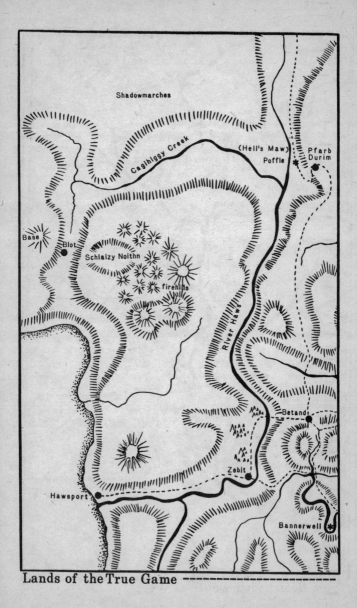

Lands of the True Game

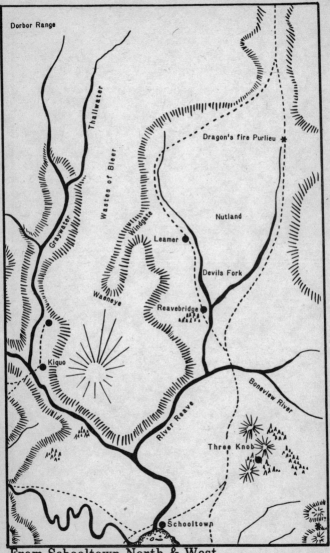

Dorbor Range

Thallwater

Wastes of Bleer

Graywater

Dragon's fire Purlieu

Nutland

Windgate

Leamer

Devils Fork

Waeneye

Reavebridge

Kiquo

Boneview River

River Reave

Three Knob

Schooltown

From Schooltown North & West

NECROMANCER
NINE

1

Necromancer Nine

I had decided to change myself into a Dragon and go looking for my mother despite all argument to the contrary.

Himaggery the Wizard and old Windlow the Seer were determined otherwise. They had been after me for almost a year, ever since the great battle at Bannerwell. Having seen what I did there, they had decided that my "Talent" could not be wasted, and between them they had thought of at least a dozen things they wanted done with it. I, on the other hand, simply wanted to forget the whole thing. I wanted to forget I had become the owner—can I say "owner"?—of the Gamesmen of Barish, forget I had ever called upon the terrible Talents of those Gamesmen. I'd only done it to save my life, or so I told myself, and I wanted to forget about it.

Himaggery and Windlow wouldn't let me.

We were in one of the shining rooms at the Bright Demesne, a room full of the fragrance of blossoms and ubiquitous wisps of mist. Old Windlow was looking at me pathetically, eyes three-quarters buried in delicate wrinkles and mouth turned down in that expression of sweet reproach. Gamelords! One would think he was my mother. No. My own mother would not have been guilty of that expression, not that wildly eccentric person. Himaggery was as bad, stalking the floor as he often did, hands rooting his hair up into devil's horns, spiky with irritation.

"I don't understand you, boy," he said in that plaintive thunder of his. "We're at the edge of a new age. Change rushes upon us. Great things are about to happen; Justice is to be enthroned at last. We invite you to help, to participate, to plan with us. You won't. You go hide in the orchards. You mope and slope about like some halfwitted pawn of a groom, and then when I twit you a bit for behaving like a perennial adolescent, you merely say you will change into a Dragon and go off to find Mavin Manyshaped. Why? We need you. Why won't you help us?''

I readied my answers for the tenth time. I behave as an adolescent, I would say, because I am one—barely sixteen and puzzled over things which would puzzle men twice my age. I mope because I am apprehensive. I hide in orchards because I am tired of argument. I got ready to say these things. . . .

"And why," he thundered at me unexpectedly, "go as a Dragon?"

The question caught me totally by surprise. "I thought it would be rather fun," I said, weakly.

"Fun!" He shrugged this away as the trifle it was.

"Well, all right," I answered with some heat. "Then it would be quick. And likely no one would bother me."

"Wrong on both counts," he said. "You go flying off across the purlieus and demesnes as a Dragon, and every stripling Firedrake or baby Armiger able to get three man-heights off the ground will be challenging you to Games of Two. You'll spend more time dueling than looking for Mavin Manyshaped, and from what your thalan, Mertyn, tells me, she will take a good bit of finding." He made a gesture of frustrated annoyance, oddly compassionate.

"You have others," I muttered. "You have thousands of followers here. Armigers ready to fly through the air on your missions. Elators ready to flick themselves across the lands if you raise an eyebrow at them. Demons ready to Read the thoughts of any who come within leagues of the Bright Demesne. You don't need me. Can't you let one young person find out something about himself before you eat him up in your plots. . . ."

Windlow said, "If you were just any young person, we'd let you alone, my boy. You aren't just any young person. You know that. Himaggery knows it. I know it. Isn't that right?"

"I don't care," I said, trying not to sound merely contentious.

"You should care. You have a Talent such as any in the

world might envy. Talents, I should say. Why, there's almost nothing you can't do, or cause, or bring into being. . . ."

"*I* can't," I shouted at them. "Himaggery, Windlow, *I* can't. It isn't me who does all those things."

I pulled the pouch from my belt and emptied it upon the table between us, the tiny carved Gamesmen rolling out onto the oiled wood in clattering profusion. I set two of them upon their bases, the taller ones, a black Necromancer and a white Queen, Dorn and Trandilar. They sat there, like stone or wood, giving no hint of the powers and wonders which would come from them if I gripped them in my hand. "I tried to give them to you once, Himaggery. Remember? You wouldn't take them. You said, 'No, Peter, they came to you. They belong to you, Peter.' Well, they're mine, Himaggery, but they aren't *mine*. I wish you'd understand."

"Explain it to me," he said, blank faced.

I tried. "When I first took the figure of Dorn into my hand, there in the caves under Bannerwell, Dorn came into my mind. He was . . . is an old man, Himaggery. Very wise. Very powerful. His mind has sharp edges; he has seen strange things, and his mind echoes with them—resonates to them. He can do strange, very marvelous things. It is *he* who does them. I am only a kind of . . ."

"Host," suggested Windlow. "Housing? Vehicle?"

I laughed without humor. They knew so much but understood so little. "Perhaps. Later, I took Queen Trandilar, Mistress of Beguilement. First of all the Rulers. Younger than Dorn, but still, far older than I am. She had lived . . . fully. She had understanding I did not of . . . erotic things. She does wonderful things, too, but it is she who does them." I pointed to the other Gamesmen on the table. "There are nine other types there. Dealpas, eidolon of Healers. Sorah, mightiest of Seers. Shattnir, most powerful of Sorcerers. I suppose I could take them all into myself, become a kind of . . . inn, hotel for them. If that is all I am to be. Ever."

Windlow was looking out the window, his face sad. He began to chant, a child's rhyme, one used for jump rope. "Night-dark, dust-old, bony Dorn, grave-cold; Flesh-queen, love-star, lust-pale, Trandilar; Shifted, fetched, sent-far, trickiest is Thandbar." He turned to Himaggery and shook his head slowly, side to side. "Let the boy alone," he said.

Himaggery met the stare, held it, finally flushed and looked away. "Very well, old man. I have said everything I can say. If Peter will not, he will not. Better he do as he will, if that will content him."

Windlow tottered over to me and patted my shoulder. He had to reach up to do it. I had been growing rather a lot. "It may be you will make these Talents your own someday, boy. It may be you cannot wield a Talent well unless it is your own. In time, you may make Dorn's Talent yours, and Trandilar's as well."

I did not think that likely, but did not say so.

Himaggery said, "When you go, keep your ears open. Perhaps you can learn something about the disappearances which will help us."

"What disappearances?" I asked guardedly.

"The ones we have been discussing for a season," he said. "The disappearances which have been happening for decades now. A vanishment of Wizards. Disappearances of Kings. They go, as into nothing. No one knows how, or where, or why. Among those who go, too many were our allies."

"You're trying to make me curious," I accused. "Trying to make me stay."

He flushed angrily. "Of course I want you to stay, boy. I've begged you. Of course I wish you were curious enough to offer your help. But if you won't, you won't. If Windlow says not to badger you, I won't. Go find your mother. Though why you should want to do so is beyond me. . . ." and his voice faded away under Windlow's quelling glare.

I gathered the Gamesmen, the taller ones no longer than my littlest finger, delicate as lace, incorruptible as stone. I could have told him why I wanted to find Mavin, but I chose not to. I had seen her only once since infancy, only once, under conditions of terror and high drama. She had said nothing personal to me, and yet there was something in her manner, in her strangeness, which was attractive to me. As though, perhaps, she had answers to questions. But it was all equivocal, flimsy. There were no hard reasons which Himaggery would accept.

"Let it be only that I have a need," I whispered. "A need which is Peter's, not Dorn's, not Trandilar's. I have a Talent which is mine, also, inherited from her. I am the son of Mavin Manyshaped, and I want to see her. Leave it at that.''

"So be it, boy. So I will leave it.''

He was as good as his word. He said not another word to me about staying. He took time from his meetings and plottings to pick horses for me from his own stables and to see I was well outfitted for the trip north to Schooltown. If I was to find Mavin, the search would begin with Mertyn, her brother, my thalan. Once Himaggery had taken care of these details, he ignored me. Perversely, this annoyed me. It was obvious that no one was going to blow trumpets for me when I left, and this hurt my feelings. As I had done since I was four or five years old, I went down to the kitchens to complain to Brother Chance.

"Well, boy, you didn't expect a testimony dinner, did you? Those are both wise old heads, and they wouldn't call attention to you wandering off. Too dangerous for you, and they know it.''

This shamed me. They had been thinking of me after all. I changed the subject. "I thought of going as a Dragon. . . .''

"Fool thing to do,'' Chance commented. "Can't think of anything more gomerous than that. What you want is all that fire and speed and the feel of wind on your wings. All that power and swooping about. Well, that might last half a day, if you was lucky.'' He grimaced at me to show what he thought of the notion, as though his words had not conveyed quite enough. I flinched. I had learned to deal with Himaggery and Windlow, even to some extent with Mertyn, who had taught me and arranged for my care and protection by setting Chance to look after me, but I had never succeeded in dealing with Chance himself. Every time I began to take myself seriously, he let me know how small a vegetable I was in his particular stew. Whenever he spoke to me it brought back the feel of the kitchen and his horny hands pressing cookies into mine. Well. No one liked the Dragon idea but me.

"Well, fetch-it, Chance. I am a Shifter.''

"Well, fetch-it, yourself, boy. Shift into something sensible. If you're going to go find your mama, we got to go all the way to Schooltown to ask Mertyn where to look, don't we? Change yourself into a baggage horse. That'll be useful.'' He went on with our packing, interrupting himself to suggest, ''You got the Talent of that there Dorn. Why not use him. Go as a Necromancer.''

''Why Dorn?'' I asked and shivered. ''Why not Trandilar?'' Of the two, she was the more comfortable, though that says little for comfort.

''Because if you go traveling around as a Prince or King or any one of the Rulers, you'll catch followers like a net catches fish, and you'll be up to your gullet in Games before we get to the River. You got three Talents, boy. You can Shift, but you don't want to Shift into something in-con-spic-u-ous. You can Rule, but that's dangerous, being a Prince or a King. Or you can . . . well, Necromancers travel all over all the time and nobody bothers them. They don't need to *use* the Talent. Just have it is enough.''

In the end he had his way. I wore the black, broad-brimmed hat, the full cloak, the gauze mask smeared with the death's head. It was no more uncomfortable than any other guise, but it put a weight upon my heart. Windlow may have guessed that, for he came tottering down from his tower in the chill morning to tell us good-bye. ''You are not pretty, my boy, but you will travel with fewer complications this way.''

''I know, Old One. Thank you for coming down to wave me away.''

''Oh, I came for more than that, lad. A message for your thalan, Mertyn. Tell him we will need his help soon, and he will have word from the Bright Demesne.'' There was still that awful, pathetic look in his eyes.

''What do you mean, Windlow? Why will you need his help?''

''There, boy. There isn't time to explain. You would have known more or less if you'd been paying attention to what's been going on. Now is no time to become interested. Journey well.'' He turned and went away without my farewell kiss, which made me grumpy. All at once, having gained my own way, I was not sure I wanted it.

We stopped for a moment before turning onto the high road. Away to the south a Traders' train made a plume of dust in the early sky, a line of wagons approaching the Bright Demesne.

"Traders." Chance snorted. "As though Himaggery didn't have enough problems."

It was true that Traders seemed to take up more time than their merchandise was worth, and true that Himaggery seemed to spend a great deal of time talking with them. I wasn't thinking of that, however, but of the choice of routes which confronted us. We could go up the eastern side of the Middle River, through the forests east of the Gathered Waters and the lands of the Immutables. Chance and I had come that way before, though not intentionally. This time I chose the western side of the River, through farmlands and meadowlands wet with spring floods and over a hundred hump-backed, clattering bridges. There was little traffic in any direction; woodwagons moving from forest to village, water oxen shuffling from mire to meadow, a gooseherd keeping his hissing flock in order with a long, blossomy wand. Along the ditches webwillows whispered a note of sharp gold against the dark woodlands, their downy kittens ready to burst into bloom. Rain breathed across windrows of dried leaves, greening now with upthrust grasses and the greeny-bronze of curled fern. There was no hurry in our going. I was sure Himaggery had sent an Elator to let Mertyn know I was on the way.

That first day we saw only a few pawns plowing in the fields, making the diagonal ward-of-evil sign when they saw me but willing enough to sell Chance fresh eggs and greens for all that. The second day we caught up to a party of merchants and traveled just behind them into Vestertown where they and we spent the night at the same inn. They no more than the pawns were joyed to see me, but they were traveled men and made no larger matter of my presence among them. Had they known it, they had less to fear from me than from Chance. I would take nothing from them but their courtesy, but Chance would get them gambling if he could. They were poorer next day for their night's recreation, and Chance was humming a victory song as we went along the lake in the morning light.

The Gathered Waters were calm and glittering, a smiling face which gave no indication of the storms which often troubled it. Chance reminded me of our last traveling by water, fleeing be-

fore the wind and from a ship full of pawners sent by Mandor of
Bannerwell to capture me.

"I don't want to think about that," I told him. "And of that
time."

"I thought you was rather fond of that girl," he said. "That
Immutable girl."

"Tossa. Yes. I was fond of her, Chance, but she died. I was
fond of Mandor, too, once, and he is as good as dead, locked up
in Bannerwell for all he is Prince of the place. It seems the people I am fond of do not profit by it much."

"Ahh, that's nonsense, lad. You're fond of Silkhands, and
she's Gamesmistress down in Xammer now, far better off than
when you met her. Windlow, too. You helped him away from
the High King, Prionde, and I'd say that's better off. It was the
luck of the Game did Tossa, and I'm sorry for it. She was a pretty thing."

"She was. But that was most of a year ago, Chance. I grieved
over her, but that's done now. Time to go on to something
else."

"Well, you speak the truth there. It's always time for something new."

So we rode along, engaged at times in such desultory conversation, other times silent. This was country I had not seen before. When I had come from Bannerwell to the Bright Demesne
after the battle, it had been across the purlieus rather than by the
long road. In any case, I had not been paying attention then.

We came to the River Banner very late on the third day of
travel, found no inn there but did find a ferrymaster willing to
have us sleep in the shed where the ferries were kept. We hauled
across at first light, spent that night camped above a tiny hamlet
no bigger than my fist, and rode into Schooltown the following
noon.

Somehow I had expected it to be changed, but it was exactly
the same: little houses humped up the hills, shops and Festival
halls bulking along the streets, cobbles and walls and crooked
roofs, chimneys twisting up to breathe smoke into the hazy sky,
and the School Houses on the ridge above. Havad's House,
where Mandor had been Gamesmaster. Dorcan's House across
the way. Bilme's House, where it was said Wizards were
taught. Mertyn's House where my thalan was chief Games-

master, where I had grown up in the nurseries to be bullied by Karl Pig-face and to love Mandor and to depart. A sick, sweet feeling went through me, half nausea, half delight, together with the crazy idea that I would ask Mertyn to let me stay at the House, be a student again. Most students did not leave until they were twenty-five. I could have almost a decade here, in the peace of Schooltown. I came to myself to find Chance clutching my horse's bridle and staring at me in concern.

"What is it, boy? You look as though you'd been ghost bit."

"Nothing." I laughed, a bit unsteadily. "A crazy idea, Brother Chance."

"You haven't called me that since we left here."

"No. But we're back, now, aren't we? Don't worry, Chance. I'm all right." We turned the horses over to a stable pawn and went in through the small side door beside the kitchens. It was second nature to do so, habit, habit to remove my hat, to go off along the corridor behind Chance, habit to hear a familiar voice rise tauntingly behind me.

"Why, if it isn't old Fat Chance and Prissy Pete, come back to go to School with us again."

I stopped dead in savage delight. So, Karl Pig-face was still here. Of course he was still here, along with all his fellow tormentors. He had not seen my face. Slowly I put the broad black hat upon my head, turned to face them where they hovered in the side corridor, lips wet and slack with anticipation of another bullying. I was only a shadow to them where I stood. I shook Chance's restraining hand from my shoulder, moved toward the lantern which hung always just at that turning.

"Yes, Karl," I whispered in Dorn's voice. "It is Peter come to School again, but not with you. . . ." Stepping into the light on the last word, letting them see the death's-head mask, hearing the indrawn breath, the retching gulp which was all Karl could get out. Then they were gone, yelping away like whipped pups, away to the corridors and attics. I laughed silently, overcome.

"That wasn't nice," said Chance sanctimoniously.

"Aaah, Chance." I poked him in his purse, where the merchants' coins still clinked fulsomely. "We have our little failings, don't we? It was you who told me to travel as a Necromancer, Chance. I cannot help it if it scares small boys witless.'' My feelings of sick sweet nostalgia had turned to ones of delighted vengeance. Karl might think twice before bullying a smaller boy again. I planned how, before I left, I might drive the point home.

In order to reach Mertyn's tower room we had to climb past the schoolrooms, the rooms of the other Masters. Gamesmaster Gervaise met us on the landing outside his own classroom, and he knew me at once, seeming totally unawed by the mask.

"Peter, my boy. Mertyn said you'd be coming to visit. He's down in the garden, talking to a tradesman just now. Come in and have wine with me while you wait for him. Come in, Chance. I have some of your favorite here to drown the dust of the road. I remember we had trouble keeping it when you were here, Chance. No less trouble now, but it's I who drink it.'' He led us through the cold classroom where the Gamemodel swam in its haze of blue to his own sitting room, warm with firelight and sun. "Brrrr." He shivered as he shut the door. "The older I get, the harder it becomes to bear the cold of the game model. But you remember. All you boys have chapped hands and faces from it.''

I shivered in sympathy and remembrance, accepting the wine he poured. "You always had us work with the model when it was snowing out, Master Gervaise. And in the heat of summer, we never did.''

"Well, that seems perverse, doesn't it? It wasn't for that reason, of course. In the summer it's simply too difficult to keep the models cold. We lock them away down in the ice cellar. It will soon be too warm this year. Not like last season where winter went on almost to midsummer.'' He poured wine for himself, sat before the fire. "Now, tell me what you've been doing since Bannerwell. Mertyn told me all about that.'' He shook his head regretfully. "Pity about Mandor. Never trusted him, though. Too pretty.''

I twirled my glass, watching the wine swirl into a spiral and climb the edges. "I haven't been doing much.''

"No Games?" He seemed surprised.

"No, sir. There is very little Gaming in the Bright Demesne.''

"Well, that comes with consorting with Wizards. I told

Mertyn you should get out, travel a bit, try your Talent. But it seems you're doing that." He nodded and sipped. "Strange are the Talents of Wizards. That's an old saying, you know. I have never known one well, myself. Is Himaggery easy to work with?"

"Yes, sir. I think he is. Very open. Very honest."

"Ah." He laid a finger along his nose and winked. "Open and honest covers a world of strategy, no doubt. Well. Who would have thought a year ago you would manifest such a Talent as Necromancy. Rare. Very rare. We have not had a student here in the last twenty years who manifested Necromancy."

"There are Talents I would have preferred," I said. Chance was looking modestly at his feet, saying nothing. This fact more than anything else made me cautious. I had been going to say that Necromancy was not my own or only Talent, but decided to leave the subject alone.

"I don't think I even have a Gamespiece of a Necromancer," he said, brow furrowed. "Let me see whether I do. . . ." He was up, through the door into the classroom. I followed him as seemed courteous. He was rooting about in the cold chest which housed the Gamespieces, itself covered with frost and humming as its internal mechanism labored to retain the cold. "Armigers," he said. "Plenty of Armigers. Seers, Shifters, Rancelmen, Pursuivants, quite an array here. Minor pieces; Totem, Talisman, Fetish. Here's an Afrit, forgotten I had that. Here's a whole set of air serpents, Dragon, Firedrake, Colddrake, all in one box. Well. No Necromancer. I didn't think I had one."

I picked up a handful of the little Gamespieces, dropped them quickly as their chill bit my fingers. They were the same size as the ones I carried so secretly, perhaps less detailed. Under the frost, I couldn't be sure. "Gamesmaster Gervaise," I asked, "where do you get them? I never thought to ask when I was a student, but where do they come from?"

"The Gamespieces? Oh, there's a Demesne of magicians, I think, off to the west somewhere, where they are fashioned. Traders bring them. Most of them are give-aways, lagniappe when we buy supplies. I got that set of air serpents when I bought some tools for the stables. Give-aways, as I said."

"But how can they give them away? To just anyone? How could they be kept cold?"

Gervaise shook his head at me. "No, no, my boy. They don't give Gamespieces to anyone but Gamesmasters. Who else would want them? They do it to solicit custom. They give other things to other people. Some merchants I know receive nice gifts of spices, things from the northern jungles. All to solicit custom." He patted the cold chest and led the way back to Chance. The level of wine in the bottle was considerably lower, and I smiled. He gave me that blank, "Who, me?" stare, but I smiled nonetheless.

"I hear Mertyn's tread on the stairs," I said. "I take leave of you, Gamesmaster Gervaise. We will talk again before I leave." And we bowed ourselves out, onto the stair. I said to Chance, "You were very silent."

"Gervaise is very talkative among his colleagues, among the tradesmen in the town, among farmers. . . ." Chance said. "You may be sure anything you said to him will be repeated thrice tomorrow."

"Ah," I said. "Well, we gave him little enough to talk of."

"That's so," he agreed owlishly. "As is often best. You go up to Mertyn, lad. I'm for the kitchens to see what can be scratched up for our lunch."

So it was I knocked on Mertyn's door and was admitted to his rooms by Mertyn himself. I did not know quite what to say. It was the first time I had seen him in this place since I had learned we were thalan. I have heard that in distant places there are some people who care greatly about their fathers. It is true here among some of the pawns. My friend Yarrel, for example. Well, among Gamesmen, that emotion is between thalan, between male children and mother's full brother; between female children and mother's full sister. Here is it such a bond that women who have no siblings may choose from among their intimate friends those who will stand in such stead. But our relationship, Mertyn's and mine, had never been acknowledged within this house.

He solved it all for me. "Thalan," he said, embracing me and taking the cloak from my shoulders. "Here, give me your hood, your mask. Pfah! What an ugly get-up. Still, very wise to wear it. Chance's choice, no doubt? He was always a wary one. I did better than I knew when I set him to watch over you.''

I was suddenly happy, contented, able to smile full in his face without worrying what he would say or think when I told him why I came. ''Why did you pick Chance?'' I asked.

''Oh, he was a rascal of a sailor, left here by a boat which plied up and down the lakes and rivers to the Southern Seas. I liked him. No nonsense about him and much about survival. So, I said, you stay here in this House as cook or groom or what you will, but your job is to watch over this little one and see he grows well.''

''He did that,'' I said.

''He did that. Fed you cookies until your eyes bulged. Stood you up against the bullies and let you fight it out. Speaking of which, I recall you often had a bit of trouble with Karl? Had a habit of finding whatever would hurt the most, didn't he?''

''Oh,'' I said and laughed bitterly, ''he did, indeed. Probably still does.''

''Does, yes. Early Talent showing there. Something to do with digging out secrets, finding hidden things. Unpleasant boy. Will be no less unpleasant in the True Game I should think. Well, Chance stood you up to him.''

''I'm grateful to you for Chance,'' I said. ''I . . . I understand why you did not call me thalan before.''

''I didn't want to endanger you, Peter. If it had been known you were my full sister's son, some oaf would have tried to use you against me. Some oaf did it anyhow, though unwittingly.'' He sat silent for a moment. ''Well, lad, what brings you back to Mertyn's House? I had word you were coming, but no word of the reason.''

''I want to find Mavin.''

''Ah. Are you quite sure that is what you want to do?''

''Quite sure.''

''I'll help you then, if I can. You understand that I do not know where she is?''

I nodded, though until that moment I had hoped he would simply tell me where to find her. Still.

He went on, ''If I knew where she was, any Demon who wanted to find her could simply Read her whereabouts in my head and pass the word along to whatever Gamesman might be wanting to challenge her. No. She's too secret an animal for that. She gives me sets of directions from time to time. That's all. If I need to find her, I have to try to decipher them.''

"But you'll tell me what they are?"

"Oh, I've written down a copy for you. She gave them to me outside Bannerwell, where we were camped on Havajor Dike. You remember the place? Well, she came to my tent that night, after the battle, and gave them to me. Then she pointed away north—which is important to remember, Peter, north—and then she vanished.''

"Vanished?"

"Went. Away. Slipped out of the tent and was gone. Took the shape of an owl and flew away, for all I know. Vanished.''

"Doesn't she ever stay? You must have grown up together as children?"

"Oh, well, by the time I was of an age to understand anything, she was almost grown, already Talented. Still, I remember her as she was then. She was very lovely in her own person, very strange, liking children, liking me, others my age. She did tricks and changes for us, things to make us laugh. . . .''

"And she brought me to you?"

"Yes. When you were only a toddler. She said she had carried you unchanging, and nursed you, unchanging, all those long months never changing, so that you would have something real to know and love. But the time had come for you to be schooled, and she preferred for some reason not to do that among Shifters. I never knew exactly why, except that she felt you would learn more and be safer here. So, she brought you here to me, in Mertyn's House, and I lied to everyone. I said you were Festival-get I'd found wrapped in a blanket on the doorstep. Then I tried never to think about you when there were Demons about.''

"And I never knew. No one ever knew."

"No. I was a good liar. But not a good Gamesman. I couldn't keep you away from Mandor.''

"He beguiled me," I mused. "Why me? There were smarter boys, better-looking boys.''

"He was clever. Perhaps he noticed something, some little

indication of our relationship. Well. It doesn't matter now. You're past all that. Mandor is shut up in Bannerwell, and you want to find Mavin Manyshaped. It will be difficult. You'll have to go alone.''

I had not considered that. I had assumed Chance would go with me wherever I went.

"No, you can't take Chance. Mavin may make it somewhat easier for you to find her, but she will not trust anyone else. Here," he said and handed me a fold of parchment. "I've written out the directions.''

> *Periplus of a city which fears the unborn.*
> *Hear of a stupration incorporeal.*
> *In that place a garment defiled*
> *and an eyeless Seer.*
> *Ask him the name of the place from which he came*
> *and the way from it.*
> *Go not that way.*
> *Befriend the shadows and beware of friends.*
> *Walk on fire but do not swim in water.*
> *Seek out sent-far's monument, but do not look upon*
>   *it.*
> *In looking away, find me.*

"It makes no sense," I cried, outraged. "No sense at all!''

"Go to Havajor Dike," he said soothingly. "Then north from there. She would not have made the directions too difficult for either of us, Peter. She does not want to be lost forever, only very difficult to find. You'll be able to ravel it out, line by line. There is only one caution I must give you.''

He waited until he saw that he had my full attention, then made his warning, several times. "Do not go near Pfarb Durim. If you go to the north or northwest, do not go near that place, nor near the place they call Poffle which is, in truth, known as Hell's Maw.'' He patted me on the shoulder, and when I asked curious questions, as he must have known I would, said, "It is an evil place. It has been evil for centuries. We thought it might change when old Blourbast was gone, but it remains evil today. Mavin would not send you near it—simply avoid it!'' And that was all he would say about that.

We went down into the kitchens, sat there in the warmth of that familiar place, eating grole sausage and cheese with bread warm from the baking. It was a comforting time, a sweet time, and it lasted only a little while. For Gervaise came bustling in, his iron-tipped staff making a clatter upon the stones.

"An Elator has come, Mertyn," he cried. "He demands to see you at once. He comes from the Bright Demesne. . . ."

So we went up as quickly as possible to find an Elator there, one I knew well, Himaggery's trusted messenger.

"Gamesmaster," he said, "the Wizard Himaggery and the old Seer, Windlow, have vanished."

"Vanished?" It was an echo of my own voice saying that word, but this time we were not talking of Shifters. Mertyn asked again, "What do you mean, vanished?"

"They went to Windlow's rooms after the evening meal, sir, asking that wine be sent to them there. When the steward arrived, the room was disturbed but empty. We searched the Demesne, but they are both gone. . . ."

"Why have you come first to me?"

"Gamesmaster, I was told by the Wizard some time since that if anything untoward should happen, I was to come to you."

"Windlow told me," I cried. "Just before I left. That's what he meant when he said they would need your help soon. That word would reach you . . ."

"I warned them," Mertyn grated. "I warned them they might be next if they went on with it."

"Next?" The word faltered in my throat.

"Next to disappear. Next to vanish. Next to be gone, as too many of our colleagues and allies now are gone."

"I might have stopped it," I cried. "Himaggery told me he needed me, but I wouldn't listen. . . ."

He shook me, took me by my shoulders and shook me as though I had been seven or eight years old. "This is no time for dramatics, my boy, or flights of guilt. Be still. Let me think."

So I was still, but it was a guilty stillness. If I had been there? If I had been willing to take up the Gamesmen of Barish and use them, use the Talents? Would Himaggery and Windlow still be there? I wanted to cry, but Mertyn's grip on my shoulder did not loosen, so I stood silent and blamed myself for whatever it was that had happened.

The Skip-rope Chant	The Gamesmen of Barish, their Talents.
Mind's mistress, moon's wheel, Cobweb Didir, shadow-steel.	*Grandmother Didir, First Demon. Talent, Telepathy.*
Mighty wing, lord of sky, lofty Tamor, hover high.	*Grandfather Tamor, First Armiger. Talent, Levitation.*
Night-dark, dust-old, bony Dorn, grave-cold.	*Dorn, First Necromancer. Talent, Raising of Ghosts.*
Flesh-queen, love-star, lust-pale, Trandilar.	*Trandilar, First Ruler. Talent, Beguilement.*
Pain's maid, broken leaf, Dealpas, heart's grief.	*Dealpas, First Healer. Talent, Healing.*
Cheer's face, trust's clasp, far and strong is Wafnor's grasp.	*Wafnor, First Tragamor. Talent, Telekinesis.*
Far-eyed Sorah, worshipper, many gods who never were.	*Sorah, First Seer. Talent, Clairvoyance.*
Here and gone, flashing fast, Hafnor is trusted last.	*Hafnor, First Elator. Talent, Teleportation.*
Chilly Shattnir, power's store, calling Game forevermore.	*Shattnir, First Sorcerer. Talent, Power storage.*
Fire and smoke, horn and bell, messages of Buinel.	*Buinel, First Sentinel. Talent, Fire starting.*
Shifted, fetched, sent-far, trickiest is Thandbar.	*Thandbar, First Shifter. Talent, Shapeshifting.*
When all time is past, eleven first, eleven last.	The eleven represent the pantheon of elders, the "respected ones" of the religion of Gameworld.

NOTE: There are short verses for every Gamesman in some issues of the Index of Gamesmen, over four thousand different titles. In some areas, skip-rope competitions are held during which young men and women attempt the recitation of the entire Index. The last person to complete this task successfully was Minery Mindcaster, in her eighteenth year, at the competition in Hilbervale.

2

A City Which Fears
the Unborn

At the end of the short time which followed, it was Mertyn who left me, not I who left him. I had never seen him in this kind of flurry, this Kingly bustle with all the House at his command and no nonsense about not using Talents in a Schooltown. He simply ordered and it was done, a horse, packing, certain books from the library, foodstuffs, two Armigers and a young Demon to accompany him. I did nothing but get in his way, each time trying to tell him that I would go back with him to the Bright Demesne to do what I should have done in the first place. He would have none of it.

"For the love of Divine Didir, Peter, sit down and be still. If there were anything you could do, I would have you do it in a moment. There is nothing. Believe me, nothing. Just now the most important thing you can do is what you were intending to do anyhow, find Mavin and tell her what has happened here. Give me a moment with these people and I'll talk to you about it. . . ."

So I sat and waited, with ill grace and badly concealed hurt. It was quite bad enough to remember that I had come away when I was needed; it was worse now to be denied return when I was eager to help. At last Mertyn had all his minions scattered to his satisfaction, and he came back to me, sitting beside me to take my hand.

"Thalan, put your feelings aside. No—I know how you feel.

19

You could not have failed to love old Windlow. All who know him do. As for Himaggery, it is hard not to like him, admire him, even when he is most infuriating. So, you want to help. You can. Hear me, and pay utmost attention.

"For some time there have been disappearances. Gamesmen of high rank. Wizards. Almost always from among those we would call 'progressive.' Many have been Windlow's students over the years. It can't be mere happenstance, coincidence. We suspect the cause but have no proof.

"Are those who have vanished dead? If they are, then some among the powerful Necromancers should be able to raise them, query them, find out what has happened. So, Necromancer after Necromancer has called into the dust of time, but none of the vanished rise. Instead, for some few of the searchers, it has been Necromancer Nine, highest risk, and they have vanished as well. Gone. Not dead, Or, if dead, dead in a way no others have ever died." He shivered as though cold. "If not dead, then where? Demon after Demon has sought them, and for some of them it has been Demon's Eyes Nine; they have disappeared as well. Are they imprisoned? Pursuivant after Pursuivant has searched, Rancelmen have delved. We find nothing. Those who vanish are simply *gone*.

"Yet still we pursue our goal, our studies. Himaggery. His allies. Windlow's old students. Though our allies vanish, our numbers continue to grow—slowly, too slowly. I warned Himaggery to draw no attention to himself. Bannerwell was a mistake, though we had to do it. As Windlow would say, it was morally correct but tactically wrong. So it has happened. Old Windlow evidently had some foreknowledge of it; he told you I would be needed. Well, I will go and try to hold things together while you seek out Mavin because we need her. We need her clever mind, her hidden ways, her sense of strategy. You can help most by finding her, which you would have done in any case."

I could not be so discourteous as to argue against that. He meant what he said. It was no mere sop for my comfort. I swallowed my pride and assented, sorrowing that I had refused help earlier and that it was now too late. He pulled me close, whispering.

"Thalan, mark me. You have the eidolon of Dorn. I know

you dislike using it, but if you have chance to do so, query among the dead for Himaggery and Windlow. If you—by any chance—use others of those Talents—no, don't say anything, boy—seek for Himaggery and Windlow. Even half answers are better than no answers at all.''

He kissed me and went. I was left in his aerie alone, among the tumble of packing, things half out of boxes, paper scattered upon his table, maps curling out of their cases, a disorder which spoke more harshly than words of his state of mind. I spent an hour setting it right, then went to make my own preparations and to take farewell of Chance.

It was not easy. He did not accept that I would have to go alone. He could accept only that Mertyn had so ordered, and he was as bound by that order as I. At the end he told me he would go back to the Bright Demesne to await my return. He said that two or three times, to await my return, as though by saying it he could assure it would be so. It comforted me more than it did him, I'm sure. Perhaps he intended it so. I was very uncertain of what was to happen next, so preoccupied I paid no attention at all to Karl Pig-face and by my contemptuous silence (for so he and his followers interpreted it) did his unpleasant reputation grave and permanent harm. At the time, I didn't think of him at all.

I rode out of Schooltown at first light. It was a three-day trip to Bannerwell from the town. I made it in two, riding late and rising early, paying no attention to the scenery and eating in the saddle.

Havajor Dike lay just east of the fortress of Bannerwell. I came upon it at evening, late, with only an afterglow in the sky where the high clouds still shed a little reflected light. A star shone above the clouds, only one, trembling like a tear in the sadness of dusk with its blue-brown scent of dark, bat-twittered and hesitant. I saw one lonely figure upon the Dike, black against the glow, and rode up to ask what housing might be available for the night. As I came closer, I saw that it was Riddle, Tossa's father, that lean Immutable who had come to Bannerwell with Chance and Yarrel at the very end of the battle, making battle unnecessary.

It struck me when he turned to face me that he showed no fear at all. No stranger had confronted me since I had left the Bright

Demesne without showing some shrinking from me, perhaps a curious, awed stare followed, more times than not, by the "ward-of-evil," by an over-the-shoulder stare as he hurried away. Riddle had no fear, but it was a few moments before I realized that he did not know who I was and that it did not matter. He was an Immutable. They did not fear the Talents of Gamesmen, not even of Necromancers.

"Do I know you?" he asked, leaning on the wall, gaze burrowing at my gauze-wrapped face. "Have we met?"

"It's Peter, Riddle," I said, pulling the hood from my head and running dirty fingers through my dirtier hair. "I should have spoken."

"Peter." He gave me his oddly kind smile, reached out to touch my face as though I had been his child or close friend. "To see you dressed so. I had forgotten you had this . . . Talent. I thought it was something to do with . . . changing shape."

I started to say something about the Gamesmen of Barish, caught myself and said nothing. No one knew of the Gamesmen but Windlow and Himaggery, Silkhands, Chance—one or two others who would say nothing about them. Instead of explaining, I shrugged the question away. "Small reason for you to remember. I did not stay long here at Havajor Dike once Bannerwell was overthrown. Have you played jailor here alone since then?" I knew the Immutables had intended to stay at Bannerwell long enough to assure there would be no more of Mandor's particular kind of threat, but I had not expected Riddle himself to stay among them. He was said to be their leader, though I had never heard him claim any such title.

"No," he replied. "They sent for me after Mandor died."

"Dead? Mandor?" I could not imagine it, even though I had foretold it myself. I had known he could not long withstand the pain of a disfigurement visible to everyone, of loss of power, of the absence of adoration, not he who had lived for power and adoration and had adored himself not least among them. And yet . . . it was strange to think of him dead. "How did he die?"

"From the tower." Riddle indicated the finger of stone which gestured rudely from the western edge of the keep. "He stood there often. We saw him in the dusk, or at dawn, a black blot against the sky. Then one morning he was not there, and his body was found among the stones at the river's side. They sent for me then, and I arrived in time to learn that Huld had gone as well.''

"Dead?''

"I fear not.'' He looked angry, biting off the words as though they tasted bad. "Himaggery had left Demons here, around the edges of the place, to Read if any tried to escape. They did not Read Huld. I theorize that he drugged himself into unconsciousness after hiding in a wood wagon or some such. Certainly he went past us all without betraying his presence.''

I said nothing. I did not like the idea of Huld loose in the world. I shivered, and Riddle reached out to me again.

"So, my boy. What brings you to the Dike? Was it to meet with Mandor again?''

I shivered once more. "Never. I have an errand away north of here, and the Dike is a convenient place to begin the northern journey. . . .''

"Ah. Well, you will not begin that road tonight, will you? There is time for hot food, and for a bath? Some talk, perhaps. I have not had news of the south for some time. . . .''

So I went with him to his camp, a sturdy stone house near the mill, once almost in ruins but reroofed and made solid by the Immutables and those pawns released from Bannerwell. We were waited on by quiet people with faces I thought I recognized from the time of my captivity. At my unspoken question, Riddle explained.

"These were Mandor's people, yes. Once his powers were nullified by our being here, he could not beguile them any longer. None would stay. They saw him, feared him, gradually learned what he had done to them and so began to hate him, I think. He could not bear it.''

"What had he done to them?'' I asked cynically. "More than any Gamesman does?''

"More,'' he said. "Though perhaps it was not he who conceived it. . . . No. I will say no more about it.''

I wanted to hear no more about it, though later I was to wish I had insisted. I told him of the disappearance of Windlow and of Himaggery. He withdrew into startled silence, but then told me of other vanishments he knew of. He speculated, almost in a whisper. I drank wine and tried not to fall asleep. Others of the

Immutables came in and greeted me kindly enough. They murmured among themselves while I yawned. Then we were alone and Riddle was leaning across the table to put his face close to mine.

"I have no right to ask it, Peter, but I beg a service of you. One you may be loath to give."

"I will do what I can," I murmured, half asleep.

"We need to speak with Mandor's spirit. . . ."

The sickness rose in me so that I choked on it, retching, tears pouring from my eyes as I tried not to vomit upon the table. In a moment he was putting cool water on my face, giving me a cup to drink. "How can you ask it," I gargled at him. "And why? What would you know that his ghost can tell you?"

"We have found certain . . . things in Bannerwell. After Huld had gone, our people found them and summoned me. They are . . . things which some of these pawns have reason to remember with great pain. We have studied them as best we may. We need to know what they are, how used, but more important, from whence they came. Mandor would have known. We believe they belonged to him."

"Certain things . . . ." He showed them to me. They were stored in a back room of the stone house, strange things, crystal linkages, wires, boards on which wires and crystals together made patterns full of winking lights which told me nothing. They reminded me of something . . . something. Suddenly I had it. "Riddle. Long ago—ah, not long ago. About a year. Mertyn sought to protect me from being eaten up in a Game. His servant, Nitch, sewed a thing into my tunic, a thing of wires and beads, a thing like these things. If you would know of them, ask Mertyn."

"We have done. It was Nitch who knew the doing of it, not Mertyn. Nitch has gone, gone in the night without a word."

"Vanished? Like the others?"

"No. Simply gone. Have you heard of 'magicians'?"

Where had I heard of . . . yes. "Gamesmaster Gervaise. He said the little blue Gamesmen were made by magicians, west somewhere. I had not heard of magicians before, save as we all have. At Festivals, doing tricks with birds and making flowers appear out of nothing."

"I do not think a Festival magician made these." He shut the door upon them and led me back to the table before the fire. I knew he would ask me again. I wanted to refuse. How could I refuse? Oh, Gamelords, in what guise might the spirit of Mandor rise to greet the eidolon of Dorn?

"By Towering Tamor, Riddle, you ask a hard thing."

"I know. But it is said your Talent is great. I would not ask it, save you come so fortuitously to our need. I thought of it when I saw your mask, at first, and I would not ask it if I thought it endangered you."

How could I tell him that it did endanger me? It sickened me, yes. Brought nightmares and horrors, but endangerment? Well, I would lose no blood nor flesh over it. Perhaps that was the only endangerment which counted. Riddle's daughter, Tossa, had lost her life in aiding me. I could not refuse him.

"In the morning," I begged. "Not at night."

"Certainly, in the morning," he agreed. I might just as well have done it in the dark for all the sleep I had.

We went to the pit in the gray dawn. They had not laid Mandor with his ancestors and predecessors in the catacombs beneath the fortress, and I was thankful of that. There the ghosts were as thick as fleas on a lazy dog, and I had no wish to raise a host on this day. No, Mandor lay beneath the sod in a kind of declivity a little to the north of the walls, a place fragrant and grassy, silent except for the sigh of wind in the dark firs which bounded it. Riddle let me go into the place alone, staying well away from me in order that his own, strange "Talent" not impede mine . . . or Dorn's. As I left him, he said, "We need to know whence these things came. What their purpose is. By whom made. Can you ask these things?"

I tried to explain. "Riddle, I have not heretofore questioned phantoms to know what knowledge they may have. Those discarnate ones I raised on this land before were ancient, long past human knowledge, only creatures of dust and hunger, fetches to my need."

"It is said that Necromancers are full of subtlety."

"I will be as subtle as I can." Though it would be Dorn being subtle, rather than Peter. I took the little Gamesman into my hand, fingers finding it at once in the pouch as though it had struggled through the crowd to come into my grasp. He came into me like heat, burning my skin at first, then scalding deeper and deeper, nothing wraithy or indistinct about it, rather a man come home into a familiar place. I was not surprised when he greeted me, "Peter."

"Dorn," I whispered. Before, I had been fearful. This time I was less so, and perhaps this accounted for my courtesy to him, as though he were my guest. I explained what we were to do, and he became my tutor.

"Here and here," he said. "Thus and thus." My hand reached out, but it was Dorn who pointed the finger at the grass, Dorn who called the dust and bones within to rise. Mandor had not been long dead. The ground cracked and horror came forth, little by little, the worms dropping from it as it rose. I heard Riddle on the hill behind me choking back a gasp, whether awe or fear I could not tell.

"Thus and thus," Dorn went on. "So and so."

The bones became clad in flesh, the flesh in robes of state. The head became more than a skull, then was crowned once more, until at last what had been so horrible at the end of Mandor's life became the beauty I had known in Schooltown, bright and lovely as the sun, graceful as grass, and looking at me from death's eyes.

From this uncanny fetch came a cry of such eerie gladness that my heart chilled. "Whole," it cried in a spectral voice. "Oh, I am risen whole again. . . ."

I could have wept. This wholeness was not an intended gift, and yet . . . it was one I would have made him during life if I had known how. "So and so," said with Dorn within me. "You could not have made him so or kept him so in life for any length of time."

Riddle called from the hillside, reminding me of our purpose there. So I asked it, or Dorn did, of those strange crystalline contrivances which Riddle was so concerned about. The phantom seemed not to understand.

"These are not things which Mandor knew. These are things of Huld. Playthings for Huld. Magicians made them. Huld understood them, not Mandor. Oh, Mandor, whole, whole again . . ."

I heard Riddle cursing, then he called to me, "I'm sorry, Peter. Let the pathetic thing go back to its grave."

But I was not ready to do that. I had remembered Mertyn's

words concerning those who had vanished.

"Mandor, do you speak with others . . . . where you are? Do the dead talk together?"

The fetch stared at me with dead eyes, eyes in which a brief, horrible flame flickered, a firefly awareness, a last kindling.

"In Hell's Maw," it screamed at me. "They speak, the dead who linger speak, before they fall to dust, in the pits. When all is dust, we go, we go. . . ."

"Have you spoken to Himaggery?" I asked. "To Windlow the Seer?" I remembered the names of others Riddle had told me of and asked for them, but the apparition sighed no, no, none of these.

Then it drew itself up and that brief flame lit the empty eyes once more. "Words come where Mandor is . . . troubling . . . all . . . seeking those you seek . . . not there . . . not in the place . . . Peter . . . let me be whole, whole, whole. . . ."

I sobbed to Dorn. "Let him be whole, Dorn, as he goes to rest." And so it was the phantom sank into the earth in the guise he had once worn, the kingly crown disappearing at last, in appearance as whole as he had been in Schooltown before his own treachery maimed him.

And I was left alone, Dorn gone, Mandor gone, only Riddle standing high upon the rim as the wind sighed through the black firs and the grasses waved endless farewell on Mandor's grave. Inside me a small dam seemed to break, a place of swampy fear drained away, and I could turn to Riddle with my face almost calm to go with him back to the millhouse. He was no more given to talk than I, and we had a silent breakfast, both of us thinking thoughts of old anguish and, I believe, new understanding.

When we had eaten he said, "Peter, I will go with you a way north. I have an errand in that general direction, and it is better never to travel alone. That is, if I am welcome and my own attributes will not inhibit your . . . business."

I laughed a little. "Riddle, my business is a simple one. I am going in search of my mother who has . . . left word of her whereabouts in a place known as 'a city which fears the unborn.' All I know of the place is that it is north of here."

"But, my boy, I know the place," he exclaimed. "Or, I should say, I've heard of it. It is the city of Betand, between the upper reaches of the Banner and . . . what is the name of that river? . . . well, another river to the west. I will go with you almost that far. My business will take me east at the wilderness pass.''

"Why is it called a city which fears the unborn?''

''It seems to me I heard the story, but I've forgotten the details of it. Something to do with a haunting, some mischance by a wandering Necromancer. Your Talent is not generally loved, Peter, though I can see that it may be useful.''

He was being kind, and I helped him by changing the subject. I was glad enough of his company, gladder still when he proved to be a better cook than Chance and almost as good a companion as my friend Yarrel had been when we were friends. On the road we talked of a thousand things, most of them things I had wondered at for years.

One of the things that became apparent was that the Immutables cared little for Gamesmen. Riddle's toleration of me and of a few others such as Himaggery was not typical. I asked him why they let Gamesmen exercise Talents at all, feeling as they did.

''We are not numerous enough to do otherwise,'' he said. ''There are fewer Immutables than there are Gamesmen, many fewer. We do not bear many children, our numbers remain small and our own skills remain unchanging through time— Immutable, as you would say. Each of us can suppress the Talent of any Gamesman for some distance around us. I can be safe from Demons Reading my thoughts or Armigers Flying from above, but I am not safe from an arrow shot from a distance or a flung spear, as you well know.''

I nodded. Tossa had died from an arrow wound.

''So, those of us with the ability find it safer to band together in towns and enclaves with our own farms and crafters. Thus we can protect ourselves and our families from any danger save force of simple arms, and this we can oppose with arms of our own. We could be overrun, I suppose, if any group of Gamesmen chose to do so, but Gamesmen depend too much upon their Talents. Without the Talent of Beguilement, few if any of their Rulers would be able to lead men into battle. And, of course, the pawns will not fight us. They turn to us for help from time to time.''

''I would think all pawns would flock to you for protection.''

"We could not protect them. We are too few."

"What do they want, you want, Riddle? The Immutables?"

"We want what any people want, Peter. We want to feel secure, to live. We want to be free to admire the work of our own hands. Even Gamesmen do the same. Why else their 'schools' and their 'festivals'? The Gamesmen depend upon the pawns for labor, for the production of grain, fruit, meat. If we were numerous enough to protect the pawns, and if they came to us, then . . . then the Gamesmen would fight, even without their Talents."

"They could till the soil themselves," I offered, somewhat doubtfully.

"Would they?" asked Riddle. Both he and I knew the answer to that. Some few would. Some few probably did, out of preference. As for the others in their hundreds of thousands, they would rather die in battle than engage in "pawnish" behavior.

So we rode together, I in the circle of his protection, he in the circle of fear which came with the Necromancer's garb. No one bothered us. There was little traffic upon the road in any case, and those we encountered left a long distance between themselves and us.

"The things you found in Bannerwell," I asked. "Why are you so curious about them?"

"I am curious about anything subtle and secret, Peter. It is difficult to keep secrets among Gamesmen. A powerful Demon can learn almost anything one knows, can dig out thoughts one does not know one has. How then are secrets kept? You would not deny that they are kept?"

"One has one's own Demons to guard against thought theft by outsiders. One stays in one's own purlieus, in one's own Demesne. . . ."

"Ah, but walls of that kind can be breached, or sapped. No. Sometimes secrets are kept, even by those who go about the world in the guise of ordinary Gamesmen. There were secrets kept in Bannerwell. Someone there *knew* things that others do not. Huld, it seems. How did he manage that. . . .?

"Do you know," he went on, suddenly confidential, "as a child I envied the Gamesmen. Yes. I was much enamored of Sorah. A Seer. How wonderful to see the invisible, the inscrutable, the future . . . how wonderful to know *everything*!"

"I don't think that's quite how it works," I said, remembering old Windlow and his frustration at partial visions of uncertain futures.

"Perhaps not. Still. There are many things I want to know. For example, does the name 'Barish' mean anything to you?" His tone was casual, but he watched me from the corner of his eye.

I took a deep breath, hiding it, wondering what to say. "Barish? Why, it's a name from religion. A Wizard, wasn't he? Did something very secret and subtle—I forget what. . . ." I waited, scarcely able to breathe. "Is it a name I should know?"

"Secret and subtle." He mused. "No. Everyone knows that much, and seemingly no one knows more than that." He smiled. "I am merely interested in secret and subtle things, and I ask those who may know. I have heard, recently, of this Barish."

I turned my hand over to let his words run out. "I do not know, Riddle. You riddle me as you must riddle others. Do you always ask such questions?"

"I talk to hear my voice, boy. I tie words on a journey as a woman ties ribbons on her hat."

"Do they?" I asked, interested. "I have only seen ribbons on students' Tunics, come Festival."

"Oh, well, Peter. You have not seen much." And with that, he lapsed into a long, comfortable silence. It had rained betimes and we found lung-mushrooms all along the sides of fallen trees. Riddle cut away a nice bunch of them, glistening ivory in the dusk, and rolled them in meal to fry up for our supper. He told me about living off the countryside, more even than Yarrel had done. Riddle spoke of roots and shoots, berries and nuts, how to cook the curled fronds of certain ferns with a bit of smoked meat, how to bake earth-fruits in their skins by wrapping them first in the leaves of the rain-hat bush, then in mud, then burying the whole in the coals at evening to have warm and tender for the morrow's breakfast.

Our road cut across country between loops of the River until the land began to rise more steeply. Then the River ran straight or in long jogs between outcroppings, plunging over these in an hysteria of white water and furious spray. Our horses climbed, and we strode beside them for part of each morning and each afternoon so they would not tire or become lame. Stone lanterns along the way began to appear, at first only broken, old ones, half crumbled to gravel, but later newer ones, and then ones lit with votive lights.

"What are these?" I asked. "Burning good candles here in the daylight?"

"Wards against the Gifters," said Riddle. "The people here-abouts are most wary of Gifters and what Gifts they may make to the unsuspecting."

"Why have I never heard of them until now?"

"Because students hear of very little." He did not make it a rebuke, but I was offended nonetheless.

"We were taught morning to evening. They did nothing but teach us of things. . . ."

"They did nothing but teach you of *certain* things, " Riddle replied sternly. "And they told you nothing of other things. They told you nothing of the Gifters, though the world north of the Great Bowl goes in constant fear of them. You are told nothing of the nations and places of this world, but only of the small part you inhabit. . . ."

"Riddle." I was caught up in a curious excitement. "Why do you say 'this world'? Do you believe it is true what the fablers say, that there are more worlds than this?"

"There are stories of others. Not that the stories are necessarily true. But that is part of what I mean. In the Schools you are all taught so little about what really is and what may truly be."

"Why would they do that? Why would my own thalan, for example, fail to teach me things I would need to know?"

"Because they do not believe you do need to know," he replied in exasperation. "They think the least told, the least troubled. If you do not hear of the Northern Lands, you will not venture there. If you do not hear of Gifters, you will not fall prey to one. It is all arrant nonsense, of course. Pawner caravans pick up a hundred ignorant youths and carry them away north for every one who adventures there on his own. Gifters make between-meal bites of the naive, while the well-taught escape with their lives. I have even heard old Gamesmen speak with tears in their throats of the 'innocence' of youth. 'Innocence,' indeed. They should say arrant ignorance and be done with it."

He fumed for another league and I did not interrupt him, for I of-

ten learned much by letting him burble. Thus it was I did not ask
him more about Gifters when I should have done.

"There is a pawnish settlement in the south," he said at last,
"in which they do not teach their children anything of sex. It is
kept a great mystery. The belief of this sect is that this ignorance
will keep their children from harm. As a result, they value vir-
ginity highly and it is virtually unknown among them."

I did not believe this, but allowed it to stand unchallenged as
we rode on. I didn't ask about Gifters, or the northlands, or anything else. Ah well. Yestersight is perfect, so they say.

We had been several days on the road when we came to a rolling range of hills and began to track upward by repeated switch-
backs, higher and higher, the way becoming more rocky and
precipitous as we went. I was reminded a bit of the road from
Windlow's House to Bannerwell, except that this one did not
seem to run through wilderness. There were villages all along
the way, cut into the sides of the mountains with meadows the
size of handkerchiefs spread upon the ledges, and a constant
procession of lanterns, little ones and big ones, never seeming
to run out of candles. At last we came to a high pass at which the
road split, one fork leading downward to the north, the other
winding to the east among the crags.

"Well," he said to me. "We are near Betand. We come to
the parting of ways, Peter. I am thankful for your company thus
far. If you will slit your eyes you will see the roofs of the city
away to the northwest, and I wish you well in your journey."

I was sorry to part from him. Truth to tell, I had never been
really alone before the brief trip from Schooltown to Bannerwell, and I did not like it much. It was not fear I felt, but
something else. A kind of lostness, of being singular of my
kind. As though there were none near to greet me as fellow. Of
course, the Necromancer's hood had much to do with that.
Nonetheless, I had been grateful for his company and said so.
We sat a time there on the pass, saying nothing much except to
let one another know we would be less comfortable on the journey after we parted. At last, as I was about to run out of polite
phrases and begin to choke, he patted me upon one shoulder.

"I go east from here, to Kiquo, and to the high bridge only
recently restored though it was eighty years ago in the great cat-
aclysm that it fell. I go to seek mysteries, my boy. You go to

seek mysteries of your own. Well, then, good journey and good chance to you.'' And he went away, not looking back, leaving me to press down the further slope toward the city I could see beneath me in the westering sun of late afternoon.

Smoke lay above it like a pall through which the towers reached, like the snouts of beasts seeking upward for air. My eyes watered, just looking at it. If there were not wind before evening, it would be thick as soup in that bowl which held the city of Betand, the City which Fears the Unborn.

3

Periplus

It took several hours to reach the city, and a wind had come softly from the north to greet me as I rode by the outskirts of the place, inns and caravansaries, stables and eating houses, taverns and stews. I decided to have a meal before entering the city. There was a place there called the Devil's Uncle, and it seemed as good as any other from the point of cleanliness and better than most from its smell. The stable boy took my beast without making any signs at all, which I took either as a sign of sophistication or of total ignorance. Either many Necromancers came here or none did. It did not matter much which.

Once within, I saw a few curious faces, one or two down-turned mouths, but no ward-of-evil signs. I ordered wine and roast fowl and a dish of those same stewed ferns Riddle had fed me on the outward journey, evidently a local delicacy. They were not laggard with the food, nor was I in eating it. No one there paid me much attention until I was almost finished and had only half a glass left in the jug. Then a wide-mouthed Trader sat opposite me and showed me his palms. I raised mine courteously, and let him talk.

"Laggy Nap, fellow-traveler," he greeted me. "Trader by Talent, philosopher by inclination. What brings one so young and horridsome to the city of Betand?"

I did not know whether to be offended, which I was, or pretend to be amused. I chose the latter as having the lesser consequence.

"Merely one who would travel through Betand on his way to

somewhere else," I said. At which he laughed, repeating my remark to some others who also laughed. I supposed there was something entertaining in the intent to travel through Betand, so ordered wine for those around and asked, all innocence, if the city were accounted so amusing by all who went there.

"Oh, sir," said the Trader, "it is my amusement to ask new wanderers whether they intend to go through Betand, and then to offer them a meal at my expense at the Travelers' Joy, which is on the other side of the city. You can tell me then whether you were amused, and I will be entertained by your account." He fixed a glittering eye upon me, seeming to look further than I would have wished. He was a man with down-slanting brows and deep furrows between his eyes, wide-mouthed, as I have said, with a long, angry-looking nose against which his eyes snuggled a bit too closely. His eyes belied his mouth, the one being all motion and laughter while the others were cold and full of accounts.

"You do not wish to tell me why I will be . . . amused?" I asked him. He merely chuckled, elbowed some of those around him, and together they engaged in laughter of a mocking sort. Almost my hand sought Dorn in the pouch at my belt, but I decided against it. No point in stirring up trouble. I took my leave of them and went on toward the walls, a gaping gate full of torchlight before me.

I began to identify myself, to give some sort of name such as "Urburd of Dowes" or "Dornish of Calber." Chance and I had made up a whole list of them to be used as needed. The guardsman gave me no time. He laid a hand upon my arm and said intently, "Sir, you are nobody here. If you would not be charged with a grave offense, remember that. You are nobody."

He passed me on to another guardsman who gazed me in the eye with equal intensity, seeming unafraid of the death's-head. "Who are you now, sir?"

"I am . . . nobody?" I said, wondering what fools' game they played and whether I was the fool for playing it with them.

"Surely, surely," said the second guardsman. "Go through this gate, sir. Leave your horse in the stables there. The matron will meet you."

He had no sooner spoken, directing me to a little postern gate in the rough wall, when there came a howling out of the night as though a chase pack of fustigars was lost in a lonely place and crying for their kind and kindred. He blanched, made the sign of evil-ward, thrust his hands over his ears. I, too, sought to block my ears, for the cry went up in a keening scream, up and up into an excruciating silence. "Quickly." He pushed me. "Go!"

I went. The woman who met me on the other side was plump and motherly, hands thrust beneath her apron, chivvying me along as though I had been her pet goose.

"Well sir," she said. "What kind of woman would you prefer? There are several in the waitinghouse tonight. Three I would call a bit matronly for you, for you walk like a lad no matter the horrid face on you. Necromancer or no, boy you are, or I'll eat my muffin pan. Well, not them, then. I've one virgin girl scared out of her wits. You'd do me a favor, you would, to take that one. Nice enough she is, but as unschooled as any nit and vocal along of it. . . ."

I had no idea what she was speaking of. "I would be glad to do you any service, madam."

"Good enough, then," she said, stopping at the first door and opening it only long enough to call within. "Sylbie, come out here, lass. Nobody is here."

A small time passed before the girl came out, a pale girl with soft brown hair and eyes swollen with crying. She gave me one glance and shrieked as though ghost bit.

"Oh, stuff and foolishness," said the Matron. "Sylbie, it is only a guise. Come now, you've seen Gamesmen all your life. Must you scritch at the lad, and him only a boy (as I can tell by his walk) to make him sorry he said he'd favor you? You could go back and wait for one of those drovers to quit drinking in the Devil's Uncle would you rather. . . ."

"N-n-no, Madam Wilderly," she stuttered. "It's only that it was very unexpected. . . ."

At that the howling began again, and we all leaned against the stone as it rushed on us out of the empty streets, shrieking and moaning, then dwindling away down the throbbing alleys once more. It was a horrid sound.

"The unborn," said the Matron in explanation. "We are haunted, sir, as you must have heard."

"I had heard," I said weakly. I had, too, but the reality made the stories dim. I would have gone mad if I had had to listen to that howling for more than a short time. These thoughts were halted by the matron's instructions.

"Just in there, sir, Sylbie. You'll find a nice room to the left at the top of the stairs. Wine all warm by the fire and a bit of supper to help you get acquainted. The Midwife will be around in the morning, just to check has the law been complied with." And with that she was off down the street in the direction we had come.

The girl led me up the stairs, I still wondering what went on. The girl seemed to know, and I assumed she would tell me. Besides, once within a room I could take off the death's-head mask and wash my face, thus showing her a face which would not frighten her. I did so, and when I took the towel away, she handed me a cup of wine. She was no longer crying, but she looked frightened still.

"Well," I said. "Suppose you tell me what all this Game is, Sylbie. I will not harm you, so you need not make dove's eyes at me."

"Don't you know?" she asked. "About Betand? I thought everyone for a thousand leagues around must know about Betand."

"Well, I did not. Even the man I was traveling with, who had heard of Betand, was not sure of the cause of its fame. You are referred to in our part of the world as 'The City Which Fears The Unborn'. Not very explanatory."

"Oh, but very descriptive, sir. It is the unborn you heard howling in the streets. It has driven some mad and others into despair. My own mother tried to drown herself from the constant horror of it. We cannot sleep by night because of the howling, and we cannot sleep by day or we will all starve. I, myself, think it might be better to starve. My father said he would rather starve than have me raped, but my mother said nonsense, the girl must be raped because it is the law."

I dropped the cup and heard it echo hollowly from under the bed where it rocked to and fro making clanking sounds. "Raped! By whom?"

"By you, sir. Or, rather, by nobody."

I sat upon the side of the bed and reached for the cup with my foot. "Sylbie, pour more wine. Then sit here beside me and tell me what you have just said. I am quite young, and I do not understand anything you have said."

"Oh, sir," she said, falling to her knees to fetch the cup, "truly you are very stupid. I have already told you. But I will tell you again.

"It was two years ago last Festival that the Necromancer came to Betand. He was an old man, and he amused the crowd at the Festival by raising small spirits (some said it was forbidden for him to do so during Festival, and was the cause of all our woe) which danced and sang like little windy shadows. Well, one night he was drinking at the Dirty Girdle, a tavern which, my mother says, has a well deserved reputation, and he got into an argument with the tavernkeeper, a man as foul of mouth as his kitchen floor, so says my mother. Doryon, the Necromancer, would not take besting in any battle of words, so my father says, and so decided to place a haunting upon the tavern. He was very drunk, sir, very drunk.

"So he rose to his feet and made some gestures, speaking some certain words, at which, so my father says, the whole company within the place trembled, for he had summoned up a monstrous spirit which fulminated and gorbled in the middle of the air, spinning. Then, so my father says, did the old Necromancer clutch at his chest and fall like an axed tree down, straight, stiff as a dried fish and dead as one, too.

"But the haunting he had raised up went on boiling and fetching, sir, growing darker and more roily until at last it began to howl, and it howled its way out of the tavern and into the streets of Betand where it has howled and howled until this night."

"But," I said, "why was not some other Necromancer brought to settle the revenant? What one can raise, surely another can put down. Or so I have always been taught."

"Sir, it was thought so. But Doryon was very drunk, and the Necromancers who came after said he had raised no dead spirit from the past but had, instead, raised up some spirit yet unborn, twisted in time and brought untimely to Betand. None of them knew how to twist it out of being and into the future again."

"So. And so. And so what is the what of that?" I was baffled, mystified. "What has that to do with being raped because it is the law?"

She shook her head at me as though I should have seen the whole matter clearly by this time. "If it is the spirit of one unborn, then it is in the interest of the city that it become born as soon as possible. Which means that every woman of Betand able to bear must bear at every opportunity."

"But rape," I protested feebly. "Why?"

"Because all sexual congress except between married persons is defined as rape in the laws of Betand. Marriages cannot be entered into lightly for mere convenience. There are matters of property, of family, of alliance. It takes years, sometimes, to work out the agreements and settlements and the contracts."

"So they expect *me* to rape you, to break the laws of the city?"

"Oh, truly you are *very* stupid, sir. *Nobody* will break the laws. Did they not say you were *nobody*? How can nobody break a law? It is manifestly impossible, so says my mother. We of Betand do not change our laws readily, so says my father, but we interpret them to our needs."

"I see. At least, I think I see." I was not sure, but it had begun to make a weird kind of sense.

"I hope so," she said, wearily taking off her jacket. "You look far less dirty than the drover." Removing her blouse, "That is, if one may choose among nobodies."

My throat was dry. I could think of nothing to say to her, nothing at all. While I poured wine and drank it, she removed all of her clothing except a filmy thing which began halfway down her front and ended above her knees. It did little to hide the rest of her. Knowing my history, you will believe it when I say she was the first female person I had seen so unclothed. Silkhands the Healer, even when she traveled across the country with us, had never been so unclad. Now that she was bare, Sylbie seemed not to know what to do next. I offered her wine, and we gulped at it together, each as uncomfortable as the other.

"Have you had lots of women?" she whispered in a voice which seemed hopeful of an affirmative answer.

I managed to say, "Ummm," in a vaguely encouraging tone.

"I didn't want to be—fumbled at," she said through tears.

"Ummm," sympathetically.

"I think it might help if I knew your name."

"P—Peter."

"Well, Peter, it's a comfort that you know about . . . every-thing. My mother says that will make it much easier," she said, then she threw herself sobbing onto the pillows.

I was—am a fearfully stupid person. Until that instant I had not considered the Gamesmen of Barish which were in the pouch at my belt. Among them was the eidolon of Trandilar, great Queen, Goddess of beguilement and passion. I had taken that eidolon once before, outside the shattered walls of Bannerwell. I had not thought of it since, had rejected use of it, had tried to pretend it had never happened. Now, faced with the sodden misery before me, I could not in conscience ignore Trandilar longer. Peter, rude boy, would indeed "fumble at her." Only Trandilar offered any hope for something less than agony for us both. My hand found the Gamespiece without try-ing, as though it rushed into my hand. I knew then what to do and how to do it as the lizard knows the sun.

"Come," I said to the girl, laughing. "Let us have some of this good supper the matron has left us. Tell me about your fam-ily. Eyes like yours are too lovely to spoil with tears." (Was this Peter speaking? Surely. If not Peter, then who? Nobody?)

Tears were wiped away. Wine was drunk and food eaten; fire allowed to warm skin to a roseate gleaming. Bodies allowed to huddle together for comfort when the howling came, to seek the softness of the mattresses and quilts, to burrow, explore, touch, wonder at, murmur at. Alone, I would have made all stiff, com-plex, and hateful, but with Trandilar all merely occurred. I seem to recall some howls from within the room, but I cannot be sure. It was of no matter.

When I awoke, I found her staring at me, the tears running down her cheeks once again.

"Why are you crying? What's the matter?"

"They will arrange a marriage for me," she sobbed, "with someone awful, and it will never be like this again."

Oh, Trandilar. Is nothing ever as it should be?

Later that morning the Midwife came to the door of our room, as the matron had said she would. The dress of a midwife is red, with a white cowl and owl's feathers in a crest. She stared at me, then laid hands upon Sylbie with an expression of fierce concen-tration before shaking her head and turning away without a word. At which Sylbie turned unwontedly cheerful, as suddenly as she had become teary before.

"You must stay another night," she crowed. "Nothing happened."

I replied, somewhat stiffly, that I felt a good deal had happened, at which she was properly giggly. I had not known before that girls were giggly. Boys are, young boys, that is, in the dormitories of the schools. Perhaps girls are allowed to retain some childhood habits and joys which boys are not. Or perhaps it is only that male Gamesmen are so driven by Talent—but no. The whole matter was too complex to think out. At any rate, the matron came again to give us leave to go into the market while she arranged for the room to be cleaned and food brought in. So the day went by and another night during which I had no real need of Trandilar, and another morning with Sylbie weeping, for this time the Midwife nodded, the owl feathers bobbing upon her head. A child would be forthcoming, it seemed, and the purpose of my being a nobody had been fulfilled. We sat in the window above the street as she shed tears all down the front of my tunic.

"There is no reason to believe you will not have great pleasure with your husband," I said. Privately, I thought it unlikely unless he had been taught by Trandilar, until I remembered that Trandilar herself had been taught by someone. "Don't cry, Sylbie. This is foolishness!"

"You don't understand," she cried. "They will marry me off to someone I don't even know. Someone old, or bald, or fat as a stuffed goose. Young men don't get wives with settlements as good as I have, or so my mother says. They have not the wherewithal. Only old men have enough of the world's wealth to afford a wealthy wife. Oh, Peter, I shall die, die, die. . . ."

She was such a pretty thing, soft as a kitten, warm as a muffin. I was moved to do something for her, saying to myself as I did so that the occasion for doing helpful things should not pass me by again while I mumbled and mowed and made faces at the moon. So much I had done when Himaggery asked my help. I would not be so laggard in the future.

"Shh, shh," I said. "Be still. If I fix it so that you may marry whom you will, will you leave off crying? Sylbie, tell me you will stop crying, and I will work a magic for you.''

There were kisses, and promises, after which I went off to see the master of that place, a great fat pombi of a merchant Duke with more Armigers around him than any Gamesman needs if he is honest. It was not easy to get to see him. I needed all the Necromancer's guise to do it. He greeted me coldly, and I resolved therefore to make the matter harder on him than I had intended.

''I am told that Necromancers have tried heretofore to rid Betand of its spectre,'' I intoned. ''Without success. I come to do what others have not done, if the price be to my liking.''

He shifted in the high seat, staring over my shoulder in the way they do. He would not meet the eyes behind the death mask, as though he were afraid I would take out his life and transmit it to another realm before time.

''What price would you ask?'' His voice was all oil and musk, slippery as thrilp skins.

''One request. Not gold nor treasure. Merely that one of the people of Betand shall be governed according to my will. For that person's lifetime.'' I made my voice sinister. He would assume I wanted torture and death as my portion, being of that kind which would sooner kill anyone than give a woman joy. I know his kind—or Trandilar knew them. Yes. Perhaps that was the way of it.

''One of my people?'' He oozed for a moment, thoughtfully. ''Will you say which one?''

''Not one close to you, Great Duke. I would not be so bold. Merely an insignificant one who has attracted . . . my attention.''

He glanced at his counselors, seeing here a nod, there a covert glance. ''What makes you believe you can do what others have not?''

I shrugged, let a little anger play in my voice. ''If I do not, you will not give me my price. If I do, you will pay me. Or I will return worse thrice over. Is this reason enough?''

At which he gave grudging agreement. I insisted it be put upon parchment, signed before witnesses with the Gamesmen oath. I trusted him as far as I could kick him up a chimney.

Sylbie and I spent the day together. When evening came I went into the center of the city and called up Dorn, explaining the problem of Betand. There was deep, mocking laughter in my head, a sound as though I had my head in a bell which someone struck softly. When he had done laughing, I became his student once again. ''Inside out.'' He showed me. ''What we would have done, inverted, so, tug, pull, twist so that it becomes this shape instead of that. Oh, this would be good sport if we were drunk. See, over there, under and through, down and over, and under once more—there is your unborn, Peter. It will be born in nine months in any case. Are you sure you want to let it rest? Ah. Well then, down and over and through once more, dismissing it thus: *Away, away into time unspent. Away, away into life unused. Be still. At peace. In quiet. And done.''* Indeed, when I let Dorn go and walked forth into the streets there was only stillness, peace, and quiet.

So I went to the Duke and waited with him while his counselors wandered about listening to the stillness. Even then he would have cheated me if he could, saying that none knew whether my Talent would hold. I told him we would let my Talent summon up something else as a demonstration, and he agreed to payment.

''There is in this city the daughter of a merchant, one Sylbie, well dowered. Last night nobody begot upon her a child which she will bear, come proper season. It is my will that she be allowed to marry as she will, or not as she chooses, no matter what the cost.''

He bloated like a frog. I thought he would burst, he was so red and purple, and murmurs behind me told me that the Duke had thought of Sylbie for himself. Well and good. If she willed it, good. If she willed it not, then devil take him. I took her the parchment he had signed and told her the names of the witnesses and took oath to lay upon kindred of mine the obligation to see that the Duke's oath was fulfilled. Then there were more kisses, and more promises to remember, and I left her.

Well, it was time to make the ''periplus of a city,'' so I walked all the way around it on the ring-road inside the walls. The ''stupration incorporeal'' had been attended to, a mere word play on rape by nobody. Now I was in search of a ''garment defiled.'' In the entire journey, I found only one place that fit, the Dirty Girdle, that same tavern Sylbie had told me of. So, it being almost time for supper, I went in. The name was far worse than the place. It was a drinking place near the vegetable markets and took its name from the farmers' habit of wiping earthy hands upon the ends of their knotted girdles. The food was good, not expensive, and the people in an ebullient mood, toasting the end of the haunting, for which the Duke had been careful to take credit. When I asked whether "an eyeless Seer" frequented the place, they told me Old Vibelo would be in at dusk. So I drank and listened to the talk and waited for whomever Old Vibelo might be.

There was some talk of disappearances. A Wizard from a town away east had vanished, as well as a respected Armiger from among his people. This talk reminded me of Himaggery and Windlow, so my earlier feelings of accomplishment and self-satisfaction were much dwindled by the time the blind Seer tapped his way through the door. I greeted him kindly and offered him a meal in exchange for his company. This seemed to surprise him, but he was nothing loath to take advantage of the offer. After a few mugs I could not have stopped the flow of talk had I willed to. So, I asked him the name of the place from which he came, and how he had first come to Betand.

"Ah, that is a story." He raised his head and his toothless gums showed between curly lips. "For a man with time to listen, that is a story indeed."

I told him I had time. Since I had no idea what the next phrases of Mavin's enigmatic directions meant, it would be wisest to listen to anything he might offer, hoping that sense would come out of it. "Say away," I said. "I'll keep your glass filled."

He began talking at once, stopping only long enough to gulp more beer or put more food into his mouth.

"I was reared in Levilan," he said, "beside the shores of the Glistening Sea where Games are mostly in fun and Seers see nothing but peace. That is east of here some considerable way, Gamesman, some considerable way indeed. We have not so many of the Schools there, you understand, and many of us grow up in our own homes with family, it being a peaceful place.

"Well, peaceful is well enough, but dull, if you take my meaning. For a young fellow with molten iron in his veins and a heart set for adventure, peaceful is duller than bearable. So, when I was some twenty years in growth, with Talent as good as it was likely to get (not to say it was too great a one, ever, but good enough for some purposes) I made pact with an Explorer to go into the northlands to the headwaters of the River Flish and all the lands beyond. Have you seen an Explorer, Gamesman? Dressed all in bright leathers with a spy glass on the shoulder and a hat made of fur? Fine. Oh, my, yes but I thought that was fine. The moth wings on a Seer's mask are well enough, but for adventure I would have had an Explorer's skins every time.''

He spilled a little beer on the table and traced it with a finger into a long, wavering line. "This would be the River Flish coming from the north into the Glistening Sea. The mountains start up there a ways. There are wild tribes there, pawns who were never tamed since day the first, giant Gifters full of malice, shadow men, oh, you think of something wonderful and you'll find it there, Gamesman, be sure you will.

"So we went along and we went along, not greatly discommoded by the travel for we were young fellows all. The land got steep and then steeper yet, so that there were places we were heaving the horses up the rocks with tackle and spending a day to go a league. But at last we came to the headwaters of the river, a great swamp full of reeds and birds and scaly things that came out of the reeds at night to leave horridsome tracks. And there were biting things there, flying things, big as a finger. Twasn't long before I had been bitten near the eye, and the eye swelled shut so that I could not see on that side. Well, I was not overconcerned. A bite is a bite, and they heal, you know. Save this one did not.

"So, the way north was blocked by the swamp, so we turned away toward the west, following the sides of the hills, with me getting blinder in the eye as time went on and feverish from it, too. We had no Healer with us, more's the shame, and many a night as I lay there heaving and sweating I longed for one. Was then we were attacked by the shadow men. I never saw one, only heard their piping and fluting in the trees and felt the darts whirring by my head. Some of us they got, and some of us they missed, and those they got were dead and those they missed went on, me among them.

"Well, soon after we came upon a camp full of big men who took us in and gave us food, and seeing how shabby we were and in what bad health, gave us a chart to lead us out of trouble. While they were at it, they gave me stuff to put on the eye which they said would fix it. Came morning they went on away north to wherever they were going, and we took the chart to begin working our way back into civilized lands.

"We were fools, Gamesman, fools. Young and inexperienced and without the sense to save our necks. The chart was false and the salve for my eye was false, and when we had done with both I was blind and we were lost in the Dorbor Range somewhere, so lost we thought we'd never come out again. They'd been Gifters, you see."

"Gifters?" I murmured.

"Aye. Gifters. Devils in the guise of humankind, generous with gifts which lead only to destruction. Well, we didn't want to die, not even me, blind as a cave newt. So we worked our way south as best we could. There was stuff to eat enough. We killed mountain zeller and ate berries, and the cliffs were full of springs and streams, so it wasn't that we hungered. Then we came upon a sizable river running away south. We built ourselves a raft and let the few horses go—poor beasts, they might be living there yet if the pombis didn't get them—and floated away south.

"Then it was hell, Gamesman, sheer hell for days on end. There were rocks in the river, and falls, and taking the raft apart and hauling it around obstacles and putting it together again. Once or twice my companions spotted smoke off in the woods, but we didn't dare see who was there for fear it might be Gifters again. We just went on and went on until we came to a long, placid stretch of river, and then we curled up on the raft and slept. I think we may have slept for some days, because when we came to ourselves we were coming to the town of Zebit, some ways south of here."

"South of here," I said, puzzled. "Bannerwell is south of here."

"No, no, Gamesman. Bannerwell is south and a little east. If you go down the *west* side of the mountains, you'll come to Zebit, and it is south of here, right enough. The river makes a long curve, so we had floated by Betand in the darkness. The river I speak of flows just west of the city, here, over a low swell of hills.

"Well, they had all had enough exploring to last them a time, and I wanted only to have a Healer do something with my eyes. Those in Zebit said there was nothing they could do, but they recommended a Healer here in Betand who was said to be very powerful. So I bought a small pawnish boy to be my guide, and we crossed the river there at Zebit and found the trail into the mountains and then north to Betand. It was all nonsense about the Healer. She could do no more than the others. So, here I've stayed since, evoking small visions in return for a place to sleep or a bite to eat. The end of my great adventure, the only one I am ever to have. . . ."

I shook my head, musing, as he nodded, lost in memory and the flow of his own voice. "So," I said at last, "you came here from the south." That didn't help me at all.

"Oh, you might say so, Gamesman. But I came from the east, you know, and from the north as well. Twas my whole adventure brought me to Betand, and it was in all directions from here. . . ."

"Save west," I said, suddenly enlightened.

"True," he murmured, saddened. "I slept in the west, but I did not see it. Oh, I've seen it in visions, the sounds of metal, the green lights, the great defenders. . . ."

Would I had paid him more attention, but I did not. My question had been answered, and I was on fire to be away. So I pressed coins into his hands and left him without hearing what he was going on about. He had come to Betand from every direction except the west, therefore west was the direction I should go. I wondered briefly what guise Mavin had taken to hear the old man's tale. She may have sat in the same place, buying beer as I had done and listening to him tell the well-rehearsed story. Well. Enough of that and time to be off. I did not even really listen to his tale of the perfidious Gifters.

I left the city through the northern gate and would have ridden on at speed save for a voice hailing me from among tents and wains at the side of the road.

"Ho, traveler. And were you amused by the city of Betand?"

It was that same wide-mouthed trader I had met in the tavern to the south of the city. I remembered he had said he would meet me, but I had paid little attention. Cursing silently, I reined in and waited for him to come up to me.

"Was it interesting, Necromancer?"

"The city was not a bad city, Trader."

"Nap, friend. Laggy Nap. Oh, yes, Betand is interesting," he said and again came that lewd laughter I remembered. "Interesting to get for no cost what one must pay for in other places, hmmm?" When I did not reply, he went on, "Well, have you a story to tell?"

"None, Trader Nap. I have accomplished my business in Betand and now ride west of here. Thank you for your interest."

"Oh, more than interest, friend! Much more. Concern. Yes, true concern. We make it a practice, my fellows and I, to befriend any Gamesman traveling alone. It is a wicked world, young sir, an unconscionable world. It takes no account of youth or business. No, only with numbers does protection come. If you ride west, then you ride as we do. Come, let me introduce you to my people."

I should have ridden away, simply ignored the fellow and gone, but the habit of courtesy was still too fresh in me. Fretting at the delay, I dismounted and walked with him to the line of wains at the roadside.

"Izia," he called. "Come out and greet a Gamesman who travels alone."

She came from behind one of the wagons, came like a vision, a Priestess, a Princess, a Goddess. I am sure my mouth dropped open. We had statues in the public square in Schooltown which embodied the ideal of female grace and form. If one of them had come to life and walked, thus was Izia's walk. Her hair was black without any light in it at all. Her eyes were smudged with deep shadow. Her lips curved downward and upward in the center in that most sensuous of lines, that half smile which is a silent evocation of passion. A few days before I would not have noticed. Now I did. So much had I learned in Betand. She walked with grace, but with a slight . . . what was it? A kind of hesitation, a tentative placement of her feet, as though she had some reluctance. So she came beside the wide-mouthed man and said in a soft, neutral voice, "Welcome, traveler. Would you desire food or drink?"

"Not for me," I said hastily. I felt I had done nothing but eat and drink for several days. "Truly, and thank you. I must ride on."

"We will not hear of it." The Trader had a firm arm about my shoulders, fingers dug into my upper arm in what might have been a friendly grip but felt like the talons of a bird of prey. "Never. You will ride with us, and we with you, for our mutual protection. If you need to go now, then so will we." And with that he called instructions to some of the people in the shade of the wagons and provoked a swift turmoil of harnessing and packing. I tried vainly to remonstrate with him, to no avail. Each argument was met with firm, smiling denial, while all the time his eyes looked into my soul without smiling at all. I had never before met one who would, on no acquaintance, call me friend so often in so insistent a voice.

Well, what could I do? They were moving out onto the road, going in the way I intended to go. It was with no good grace I accompanied them, but accompany them I did. All the while the woman, Izia, moved among the horses, as I watched her broodingly, clucking to them, speaking softly to them, fingers going to the harness as she murmured into their cocked ears, submitted to the nuzzling of their muzzles. When Nap came near, the animals shied away, but they responded to her as though she had been one of them. She was dressed in a swinging, wide skirt, a tightly-laced bodice over a wide-sleeved shirt, and high gray boots of some strange metallic weave. From time to time she would bend to stroke the boots, or more—to stroke her legs through the boots, first one and then the other, almost without seeming to know she did it. I wondered, once more, at the hesitancy in her step, then decided it must be a thing common to her people, for several of those in the train walked in the same way. Probably, I thought, it was a habit peculiar to whatever land they had come from.

I cast my mind back to the time when Silkhands the Healer had spent hours and days teaching me all the Gamesmen in the Index. It had been boring at the time, but now I searched the memories to find what type of creature this Laggy Nap might be. "Trader" had been in the Index. I recalled the Talents of a Trader, to hold power, some, and to have beguilement. The dress of a Trader was leather boots, trousers of striped brown

and red, wide-sleeved shirt, and over all loose cap and tunic
broidered with symbols of whatever stuff was traded. Laggy
Nap's tunic was covered with embroidered pictures of everything from pans and lids to horses' heads; tinner to horse dealer,
he seemed a man of many trades. None of the others wore the
guise of Gamesmen. They were dressed much as the woman
was, full short trousers over the gray boots, wide shirts and
laced vests. I wondered where they came from but forbore to
ask. I did not want to talk to the Trader more than necessary. I
did not know why, could not have explained why, but the feeling was strong. It was as though I felt he could hear more in my
words than I meant, see more in my face than I cared to show. I
smiled, therefore, and nodded as he spoke to me, saying little in
return. So are fools sometimes protected by instinct when they
are too stupid to do it by wit.

So we rode out, me silent as could be, spending most of my
time watching the woman. At first it was because I thought her
so beautiful, but after a time I saw that she was not so lovely as
first glance had told me. Her nose was too long. Her mouth too
wide. One eye was a little higher than the other, and she seemed
always to have her head cocked as though waiting for the reply
to some forgotten question. Still, I could not stop watching her,
and I rode so that wherever she was in the train, I would see her
as I rode. She drew my eyes as a treasure draws a miser.

She saw that I watched her and turned her head away, not as if
displeased, but as though saddened. I had done nothing to make
her sad. There was another reason for that, and I resolved to
learn it. Whenever we stopped, she was quick among some of
the silent men to bring drink or prepare food, and I tried to talk
with her about one thing or another. It was as though she had
never learned to speak more than three words at a time. Yes.
No. May I bring? Take some . . . Her distress at being ad-
dressed was so patent that I stopped at last, pretending what I
should have pretended from the first—disinterest. It was good I
did. Nap was scowling at me when he did not think I saw him.

There were some eight wains in the train, most of them open
wagons loaded high with crates and covered with waterproofs.
One or two were fitted up as living places in which the persons
of the train might sleep and prepare their food. One was a chilly,
small wagon which breathed vapor like a dragon and contained,

so Laggy Nap said, perishable foodstuffs accounted great delicacies in the west. The wagons creaked along behind their teams, some of horses and some of water oxen, and the persons driving were silent. Izia was silent. I was silent while Laggy Nap talked and talked and talked of everything and anything and the world.

So went a day, a night, another day, and in the evening of the second day, as I went to relieve myself in a copse at the side of the road, I realized that I was being guarded. One of the persons in the train walked by the copse, and I recalled that every time I had ridden a little ahead or lagged a little behind, someone had been beside me within moments. Yes, I told myself, you knew it before. It is this which has made you uncomfortable all along. These people are not simply offering you company on the way, they are keeping you, guarding you, and would not let you go away if you tried to escape. I was as certain of it as if I had been told it by Laggy Nap himself. I lingered in the copse, within sight of the man who watched me, giving no sign I was disturbed, going over and over in my head the words Mavin had left for my guide.

"Befriend the shadows and beware of friends." She had warned me, and I had not been alert to the warning. Well. So and so. Time enough to be wary now. I adjusted my clothing and wandered back to the wagons, pausing now and then to look at a tree or a bush. Were there shadows? If so, where? I saw none, could find none, and was greeted by Laggy Nap at the fire as though I had been away for a year and we were lovers. My throat was dry as autumn grass, and I was afraid. Well, I would learn nothing to help me by silence. It was time to play their Game and hope I had time to yet win something to my benefit.

So that evening I drank with him, talked with him, told him long tales of Betand, including three thousand things which had not happened there with at least a hundred maidens who did not exist. All the while his wide mouth smiled while his eyes looked coldly into my heart. All the while I kept my eyes away from Izia, praying I had not already harmed her by my interest. Finally, I pretended drunkenness, asked him about this and that. "Have you heard of magicians?" I hiccupped to show that the question was not of importance. "In Betand they talk of . . . hic . . . magicians."

His hand twitched. I saw the jaw tighten over his smile and
Izia, where she crouched by the fire, started touching her legs as
though wounded, looking up as though she had heard an ugly
voice call her name. I put my nose in the cup and made gulping
sounds. Something wrong. Well, I would take time to consider
it later.

"Magicians," he said cheerfully. "No. I don't think I've
heard of magicians."

"Nor I before," I babbled, all bibulous naivete. "But there
in Betand they talk much of magicians. Why is that, do you
think?"

"Oh, well, it's a parochial place, after all. Most of the people
there are ignorant, superstitious. They must talk of something,
and it is amusing to talk of wonders, freaks, Gifters . . . yes,
Gifters. They talk much of Gifters, but has any one of them ever
seen a Gifter?" His eyes watched me over the top of his cup. I
met them with a stare in which no glimmer of intelligence
showed.

"No, you know, you're right!" I slapped my knee, laughed.
"No Gifters either, you think? Wonderful. Everyone lighting
candles to something which doesn't exist . . . marvelous." I
laughed myself into a long stretching movement which let me
see Izia. Yes. She still stroked her legs, still frowned into the
fire as though in pain. Well. Cold certainty seeped into me. The
man meant me no good, no good at all.

I knew I was right when he came to my blanket to offer me a
wineskin, saying, "Some of the vintage we carry to the cities
away west. Not that stuff we've been drinking. No. Something
very special. Thought you'd enjoy it." Smile, smile, smile. I
smiled stuporously in return, took the wineskin and laid it beside me.

"Generous of you, Trader. Generous. I'll have a sip of it in a
bit. Oh, yes, soon as this last bit settles." I laughed a little, let
my eyes close as though I were too drowsy to stay awake,
watching him from beneath my lids. The smiling mouth of him
snarled, then took up its perpetual cheer.

"Sleep well," he wished me. "Drink deep, and sleep well."

"Ah, yes, yes, I will. I will, indeed." If I drank his gift, I
would probably not wake, I told myself. How in the name of
Towering Tamor was I to get out of this?

A little time went by. Darkness settled. I heard someone going by the place I lay and reached out to catch an ankle. It was Izia, and she crouched beside me saying, ''What would you, fool?''

''Izia, I may be a fool indeed to ask you, but—am I in danger?''

''Oh, poor fool, you are. And I may not aid you unless I die in more agony than you have ever felt.'' She took my hand and laid it upon her boot, high upon her leg, and held it there. Long moments went by. Then I heard Laggy Nap call from the wain, call her name, once, again, and beneath my hand the boot began to burn like fire. I drew my hand away with a harsh exclamation.

''I come,'' she called in a clear voice, then knelt to hiss into my ear. ''You see, fool. We obey. We obey, obey, obey. Or we burn.''

4

Befriend the Shadows

When the camp came awake in the morning, I pretended a headache and staggering incompetence. During the long waking hours I had decided that Laggy Nap was unsure of my powers, my Talents, and would therefore probably (though not certainly) decide not to attack me directly. No, he would attempt something else, something sly and sneaking like the drugged wine I was sure he had already offered me or, if he wanted me dead, some sneaking murder. So, I decided to appear no threat to him while I found a little time to design some strategy to protect my life. I knew Izia would say nothing. In this I was correct. For the first time I was able to interpret the discipline around me correctly. It was all fear and pain, simply that. Laggy Nap had some mental link or some other control of the boots they wore. The wearer of those boots did Nap's will or burned. I was led to a remembrance of the devices which Nitch had sewn into my tunic the year before. Were not these torture boots something of the same kind? And were both not similar to the things Mandor had said were Huld's?

Well, the provenance of the things did not matter at the moment. My life did. Therefore I staggered and sweated and even managed to vomit in the bushes. Truth to tell, I felt sick enough, though it was not winesickness but strain and fear. Oh, yes, I was fearful. In the night hours I had reached for Dorn. He had come into my mind slowly, reluctantly, murmuring "Necromancer nine, Peter, Necromancer nine." I could get nothing else out of him, and I had not needed that warning that I was at grave risk. I had already figured that out for myself.

It was not long until Nap confronted me with a false smile and prying questions. Had I drunk the special wine he had given me last night? I answered with vague noddings, sick grins, avowals that one more drop of anything would have killed me indeed. He got no satisfaction, and I knew it would not be more than a few hours before he would try something again. Let him think me an idiot. I did not think much better of myself.

I needed some other Talent, and this made me fretful, weighing and discarding notion after notion. I could shift into some other form if I left my horse and all belongings behind me. I was reluctant to do that. There was a great distance still to travel, I thought. Instinct told me that Trandilar would not move Nap. He was of a kind impervious to the beguilement of others. He was also of a kind who would not be fearful of the dead. Therefore some other Talent. Not Elator, as that would lose me horse and gear, and Elators could only move themselves between known locations. I knew no location forward on the journey, so any move would lose me leagues already traveled. Armiger? Again, horse and gear lost if I flew away. The Talents of Fire? Or Healing? What good were these to me? A Demon's Talent for Reading? Perhaps, if that would let me know what was in Nap's mind. Musing thus, I rode along beside the icy little wagon, seeing the mist rise from it like the mists far behind me in the Bright Demesne. Nothing presented itself as a good strategy. All seemed forced, difficult, possibly dangerous. . . .

Then I saw the cliffs ahead of us, looming against the lowering sky, for it had been chill and rainy during the early hours and was only now clearing. Cliffs, crumbly at the rim, trailing away in long talus slopes at their bases. An idea began to form, slowly, only bones of thought still to become fleshed and finished. The sun came from behind the clouds, hot and impatient. I reached into the pouch at my belt and found the little image of Shattnir, First Sorcerer, great lady of Power. She did not speak to me as the others had done. Instead, she flowed into my veins and across my skin, bound me around with her net, tied me into her being, and began to take the heat from the sun and place it— somewhere within. I could feel it building within me, a tightness, as though my skin were stretched and swollen. I knew my eyes were bulging and my lips turning outward, puffed, but my reflection in the polished harness plate between the horse's ears showed no change in my appearance. ''Not too much,'' I begged silently. ''Enough, Shattnir, but not too much.'' She did not listen but went on taking the power from the bright sky, more and more and more, until at last I gave up waiting to explode and let her find room for it all. When I quit holding my breath, the swollen feeling abated slightly, and evidently there was room for it all for we rode so until the mountains rose across the sun to make a long, violet-gray shade for our stopping place.

· The fires were lit, the silent pawns began their evening chores and routines. Izia moved among the horses, examining their hooves, stroking their glossy hides, murmuring to them. I excused myself to go away from the camp, unsurprised when one of the booted men followed me. I did not go into the copse, however, but up the rocky slope against the cliff, stumbling a little on the scree, seeing loose bits of it slide and rattle beneath my feet with hopeful satisfaction. There was a hollow there, a place where a piece of the cliff had broken away from the main mass leaving a narrow space behind it, no larger than a closet. I eased myself within, watching my follower peering after me. Well enough.

I reached into the pouch and took the image of Wafnor into my hand, first and greatest Tragamor. I became a room into which a man with a cheerful face entered, laughing, grasping the hands of those there with a fond greeting. Almost I could hear him, ''Dorn, Trandilar, Shattnir, how well you all look. Oh, it is good to see my friends again.'' And then he was at my side saying, ''And what have we to do?''

Perhaps I told him, perhaps he simply knew. I cannot really describe what it is like. Sometimes it is like telling another person something, sometimes it is like talking to oneself, sometimes simply like knowing. Within me I felt his arms reach up, up along the cliff face, higher and higher to the rimrock fifty manheights or more above, to grasp the stones there and move them, one, two, a dozen, slowly down and down until they began to roll and fall, to tumble clacking against others, knocking, more and more, down, an avalanche of stone, toward my hidden closet behind the stone, a rumbling roar as I shrieked to the man who watched me, ''Look out! Rock fall!'' One glimpse of his face, a white oval around the round hole of a dark scream.

Then I could feel nothing and hear nothing except the grating roar of the stones. Still Wafnor reached out to them, stacking this one and that one as they fell, arranging them over me, over and around like a cave while outside the shuddering cave the stones still fell for long moments into a shattered silence.

There were cracks among the stones around me, little crevices to let in the air and the sound. Through these I could hear the whinnying of beasts, snorts, cries of men, Izia's scream as she tugged animals away from the tumbling stones. Wafnor reached out once more, across the camp to the place my horse was tethered with my pack and saddle still upon him, urged him away into the trees, out of sight of the camp, calmed the horse there to wait for me. Then Wafnor did nothing, I did nothing, and we merely waited and listened to the sounds.

"Where is he?" Laggy Nap, raging.

A voice in answer, shaky, almost hysterical. "I don't know. He was against the rock, up in there, and it came down on top of him. He screamed at me to look out. You heard him scream. It came down right on top of him . . . buried . . . covered over . . ."

"Devils take it," Nap screamed. "What started the fall?"

"Just started. Nothing. Didn't see anything. No people, nothing moving. No thunder, nothing like that. Just started . . ."

"Shadow men? Did you see shadow men?"

"Nothing, sir. Nothing at all. He screamed, and the rocks were coming down. . . ."

Nap once more, this time strident, calling in his servitors. "Get up here, you lot. We'll have to dig him out!" He sounded frantic. Dig me out? And why? This was unexpected, but Wafnor did not seem disturbed. He reached high once again, sent a few small stones cascading at Nap's feet, followed by a medium-sized boulder or two. High above I could feel Wafnor's hands upon the megalith, swaying it.

"Get back, get back. The whole wall looks to come down. Oh, why did he come up here against the wall. Izia! Did he say anything to you?"

Her voice. "You know he did not, sir. He has said nothing to me out of your hearing. And now he is dead. . . ."

"I was told to bring him," Nap snarled. "Bring him to the west, to Tallman and the mumble-mouths. How can I go empty-handed?"

"Why would they do anything to you? It is not your fault the cliff fell. It is ill luck, but not your doing. . . ."

"I have had ill luck since the Shifter sold you to me, fool. Ill luck all the years of our travel. I would you were dead beneath that rock instead of the one I was told to bring." I heard the sound of a blow, a scream, then long silence.

A man's voice at last. "Surely even they understand things that happen which are not foreseen."

"Which are nor foreseen! Yes! But which should have been foreseen. I will demand they give a Seer to serve me. Perhaps more than one. When we arrive, I will demand . . ."

"Do we continue on this road, sir?"

"No. This road goes nowhere. We came this way only to follow that troublesome Necromancer, that death's-head, that son of a loathsome toad. Oh, I came this way only to trap him, and now he is trapped too deep for me to reach! We go back to River Haws, and north almost to Hell's Maw, then west by Cagihiggy water. We can take no time for food. We go now!"

I heard a voice saying something weary and hopeless about Hell's Maw, and the sound of another blow. Then were the rattle of harness, the creaking of wheels, the voices of men and one woman dying away to the east, gone. Then long gone. I waited, not moving. Nap was tricky. He might think to leave someone to watch. Night came. I slept. Morning came, and Wafnor moved the stones aside. I was born into the world like a revenant to a Necromancer's call, squinting in the sun. When I whistled, my horse came from the trees where Wafnor had held him throughout the night. We needed water, he and I, and only when that was taken care of did we ride on to the west. I should have been cheered, but was not. My escape, my safety were shadowed by Izia's continuing captivity, and she was in my mind during the morning hours, so much so that at last I decided it would do her no good, nor me, this brooding. So, I set my mind firmly upon Mavin's words, "Befriend the shadows." Come evening, I would try to do her bidding.

The way led upward. From a lonely height I could look back along the trail to see a small trail of dust on the eastern horizon.

Was that Laggy Nap? Izia? Was there something I should have
done which I had not? Within me was a kind of consultation,
and voices came to tell me there was nothing I could have done,
not then, that there were more urgent things for me to do. Still, I
felt the queasiness of one who leaves a needful task undone.
Though I tried not to think of her, she was much in my mind.

And still in my mind in the evening. I watched from beside
my fire, waiting for evidence of shadow men. I saw nothing,
heard nothing except an occasional interruption of insect sounds
as though something might have walked among them. Morning
came, gray and dripping, and I rode on west to another evening
and another fire. I reached out to Trandilar, begged her for a
blandishment, a beguilement to charm birds, small beasts,
whatever might be within sight or smell of me. She let it flow
through me and breathe into the air, a perfume, a subtle fragrance of desire. Watching quiet greeted it, a silent attention. I
could not say how I knew they were there, but I knew it. I slept
at last, weary with waiting for them to come to me.

In the morning I journeyed beside a stream which became a
small river. I had come high onto a tilted upland that slanted
down toward the west, and the river I followed was fed from all
sides by swiftly flowing rivulets making conversational noises
over the polished stones of their beds. By day's end I began to
smell something strange, a vast wetness, like that of the Gathered Waters, but different in some way I could not describe.
Suddenly, the air before me was full of rainbows, the river
plunged away through a notch in the land, and I could see the
waters below, a mighty sea stretching beyond sight into the
west. The evening wind was in my face, thrusting the waters
onto the beach below in long combers of white. A twisting path
wound down the face of the cliffs, and at the bottom the beaches
reached away north and south in a smooth curve into which the
elevated land behind me dropped and vanished. Some little distance to the north was an inlet bordered with trees, a grassy
bank, a pool of still water over which white flowers nodded
their heads and devil's needles dipped glassy wings. The horse
stumbled with tiredness; I licked lips wet with salt and almost
fell when I dismounted. There was no sound but water talk, yet I
knew something was watching me, had been watching me for

days. I was too weary to eat so only pulled the saddle from the horse and rolled myself into a blanket to sleep dreamlessly.

It was dark when I woke, dark lit by a half moon. Some sound had wakened me, some cry. I stared across the moonlit waters to see a boat, a long, low boat like those carried on larger ships. It seemed empty, but I had heard a cry. The boat showed only as an outline against a kind of glow, a subtle luminescence, nebulous and equivocal. It drifted toward me, grated on the pebbles of the beach and rocked there, each wave threatening to carry it out once more. In my sleep-befuddled mind it seemed fortuitous, a boat to carry me west. I stumbled out of my blanket, still half asleep, intending to pull the boat further onto the shore.

Then, as I stumbled toward the boat, an anguished keening came out of the dark, and I was stopped, unable to move further. There were little arms about my legs, thrusting me back, tugging at me, moving me away from the boat. Between me and the impalpable glow, I could see their figures outlined. Two or three of them carried something among them, a balk of timber perhaps—something bulky. They went close to the boat, heaved their burden high and ran wildly away. The bulky burden fell within the boat. . . .

And the boat tilted upward, rose into the air, became the end of an enormous pillar to which it was attached, a monstrous, flexible arm upon which it was only a leaf-shaped tip, one among many mighty tentacles thrashing upward in a maelstrom of sinew to tangle themselves around the "boat" and carry it beneath the surface. The little fingers pushed me back, back, and from the waters those tentacles came once more, questing across the pebbles with palpable anger to find the prey they had been denied. Against the watery glow I thought I saw a nimbus outlining an eye, rounder than the moon and as cold, peering enormously at the small shadowy figures which capered on the pebbled shore and hooted as they danced.

They were quadrumanna, the four-handed ones, shadow people, silky-furred, with ears like delicate wings upon their heads and sharp little teeth which glinted in the half light of the stars. All through the hooting and warbling they never ceased to tug at me, back away from the water's edge, back to the place I had slept. As we went they acted out the rage of the water creature, letting their long, supple arms twist like the tentacles, dropping them onto the pebbles in an excess of artful rage. "Hoo, hoo, hoor, oor, oor." Others gathered from the streamside until I was surrounded by a jigging multitude. All sleep had been driven away. I fed sticks into a hastily kindled fire, watching the celebration.

One of them brought me a fruit, which I ate, and this moved others to bring me bits of this and that, some of which smelled and tasted good, others which I could not bring myself to put in my mouth. They learned quickly. If I rejected a thing, they brought no more of it. After a time the excitement dwindled, and they gathered in crouching rows to watch me. I reached to the nearest, patted him (or her, or it) saying, "Friend." They liked that. Several mimicked my word in my own voice, and others took it up, "Friend, rend, end, end, end." At this, a silvery one from among them was moved to stand and come to my side, to strike his chest with an open hand. "Proom," he said. "Proom. Proom."

I tapped his chest, said "Proom," then struck my own. "Peter."

"Peter, eater, ter, ter," they murmured, enchanted.

The grizzled one waved at the waters, at the tremulous surface, mimed a swimming stroke, raised his hands in the writhing mime of tentacles. "D'bor."

I pointed to the waves and repeated the word. He nodded. It seemed to be going well from his point of view.

"D'bor, nonononono," he said proudly, miming swimming once more. "nonononono."

I laughed. "Nonononono," I agreed, at which we both nodded, satisfied. Mavin's words came to me. "Walk on fire, but do not swim in water." Surely. Water was a nonononono.

Well then, walk on fire I would, if I could find any. I fed sticks to the fire, building the blaze high, then stood to point both hands toward it in a hierarchic gesture before walking around it, one hand over my eyes, peering into the darkness north, west, south, and east, then pointing to the fire once more. They conferred among themselves, a quiet gabble. The grey one pointed to the fire, "Thruf," he said. Then he turned toward the north. "Thruf," he said again, indicating something big, bigger, huge.

I mimicked his mime, used his word. "Thruf," made walking motions. The soft gabbling continued among them, and several got up to come after me, following, walky-walky in the soft grass, going nowhere. They giggled. Evidently several would go with me, when I went. Time enough to go when the sun came up, or so I thought. They thought otherwise. The ones who had appointed themselves, or had been appointed, for all I knew, took up my belongings and went to get my horse, standing nose to nose with the beast as each made whiffling noises of intimate interrogation and reply. Nothing would do but that I mount the animal and go along quietly as they led him. Well enough. If I put my mind to it, I could almost sleep in the saddle. So we went, along the pebbled shoreline of the waters—though well back from the edge—toward the north. The sky grew dim, milky with dawn, and my guides showed consternation amounting almost to agitation. There was an abrupt halt to forward movement, a casting about from place to place, then a long "hoor-oor-oor" from a forested slope. The others followed it and brought me to a cavelet, dark as a nostril in the side of the mountain. They laid my belongings down, made quick forays into the wood for dry branches and twigs, piled these beside the wall of the hill, then vanished within the darkness to a trailing "hoor-oor-oor-oor." I decided this meant hello, goodbye, and here-I-am. I called softly after them. The answer was silence.

So. I was abandoned for the daylight hours. Their huge eyes and winglike ears should have told me they were creatures of the dark. I had the day before me and was not sleepy, so I went fishing. It took half the day to make a proper fish spear and half the afternoon to spear fish enough for the troop. I had a nap and built the fire up before they appeared at dusk. I was not long in doubt whether they liked fish, for there was much smacking of narrow lips, rubbing of round bellies, and hooting of a melodious kind. When they had eaten every scrap of skin and sniffed the bones several times, they urged me into the saddle once more to ride throughout the night. Again, they led while I slept, waking only a little now and again to see a changed horizon, a mountain moved from before me to behind me. I told off the days of my journey, counted them, named them over. Tomorrow, I told myself, would be rabbit day. I had little food left in the saddle bags and we had left the stream behind us.

So it went, rabbit day succeeded by dove day, succeeded by fish day II, succeeded by the day we ate greens and nuts. The little people were mightily disappointed at this, but I had had no luck at all in the hunt. We had come to a stretch of moorland crossed by tiny rivulets. There was greenery aplenty, but nothing seemed to be feeding on it but us. That night, half way through the dark hours' travel, I saw the glow of fire upon the horizon, half hidden behind a bulk of hill. Before morning it stood plain before us, fountains of fire, and behind them more fountains yet to the limits of vision. "Thruf," gabbled my escort in great satisfaction. "Thrufarufarufaruf." I presumed that this meant more fires than one.

As there were. Soon we walked among them, the glowing hills around us closer and more difficult to avoid. Flames erupted from hidden vents in the stone, liquid fire ran into crevasses to glow and breathe like embers, nearer and nearer. Soon we came to a place where there was no avoidance possible. Directly before the horse's nose a wide strip of glowing lava lay, shining scarlet in the light wind, crusted and scabbed with cinder. The horse shuddered and refused to go further. "Chirrup," said one of the shadow people importantly, pulling at my leg. "Chirrup." They pulled my things from the horse's back, handing me some of them to carry, carrying others themselves. Then, without hesitation, the chirruping four-handed one set his furry feet onto the glowing stone. Others followed, one remaining behind to hold the horse. "Walk on fire," I told myself, sweating, waiting for the pain to burn upward through the soles of my boots. Nothing. Around me the crackle of flames, but my feet were cool. "Chirrup," my guide called. "Thrufarufarufaruf."

We walked as on a road of glass. The appearance of fire was only reflection from the geysers and fountains to either side. Rivers of fire ran beside us. Heaped mountains of half molten stuff built into fantastic shapes. From these came heat as from a furnace, but upon the road we walked it was cool. We seemed to be crossing a narrow neck of the fiery land between two towering heights crowned with spouting smoke which boiled upward toward the bloody cloud, hideous and heavy with ash and rain. Before me the little ones began to run, gamboling from side to side of the way. "Chirrup, chirrup, Peter, eater, ter, ter."

An answering call came from ahead. We ventured between the last flaming fountains to emerge upon a hillside, green and cool, with a steady wind blowing the heat away and a glint of water showing among the trees. The little ones leapt on, me laboring after them, wishing I had taken time to pack properly and roll my blankets so they would not fall around my feet. As it was, I arrived in a shambling rush, half tripped up by trailing bedstuffs, red-faced from the heat and the hurry, to fall on my face before the one who awaited us. She did me the discourtesy of laughing rudely.

"Rise, Sir Gamesman," she said, sneering at the tumbled stuff around me. She turned away to hold a multisyllabled conversation with the quadrumanna which seemed to much delight them, for they giggled endlessly and rolled upon the ground clutching at themselves.

"I have asked them," she said, "if you are one of the mythical tumble-bats who roll themselves endlessly through the world not knowing their heads from their tails. They are inclined to believe this, though they say you are a good provider and are, possibly, the one whose travel was arranged for by Mavin Manyshaped. Are you indeed he?"

"She is my mother," I said wearily.

"Ah. Well then, you are he. Mavin has not so many sons that we would mistake one of them for another. Your name would be Peter?"

"Yes. And yours?"

"You may call me Thynbel, or Sambeline. Or anything else you would rather."

I grasped at the last name. "Sambeline. Did my mother arrange for you to meet me?"

"Indeed, no. She arranged for me to meet the people of Proom to pay them for their trouble in guiding you here. Though they say they are already well paid since they have your horse."

"My horse? What will they do with my horse?"

"It may be they will sell him, but I think they will eat him."

I could think of no reply to this. It was not a horse I had loved or cared for, but still, it was a good horse. A well-trained horse.

A horse which had served me well. "If you pay them, would they consent not to eat the horse?"

"It may be. Or I may pay them and they may eat the horse regardless. But I will try for you."

So she did, engaging in a lengthy and intricate argument, full of words which echoed themselves endlessly. At last the little people giggled a final round, held out their hands for their pay, and had put into those hands a wealth of silvery bells and metal flutes, bright as the sun. They clasped my legs, slapped my sides, called me "Peter, eater, ter, ter" one last time and went capering back down the trail of false fire into the distant dawn.

Sambeline waved at them, turned to me, saying, "They say they will turn the horse loose in the meadows until you return, Peter. They may do that. They may forget. They may do it and then forget and eat it later. They forget a lot, those little ones. They forget where they put their bells and flutes. They lose them by the dozens. So they are always eager for more and are willing to be paid. If they did not lose things, they would not work for us at all. Now they will have music for a time and sing many long songs of their trip to the firelands with the son of Mavin Manyshaped."

I finished packing my things into more compact bundles and strapped them together into a pack I could carry. She made no offer to help, merely sneered at these efforts. I said, "I must needs go further, but you say you are not my guide?"

"No. I will go with you a short way. You are in the land of Schlaizy Noithn, the land of the Shifters. None can guide you here. This is Schlaizy Noithn and no roads run the same here. Not for long. Where do you want to go?"

I sat upon the pack. The dawn had uncovered a green land, forested, flowing with rivers and spotted with pools and lakes. It lay beneath the height on which we stood, stretching north and west in a lovely bowl which cupped at the edge of vision to other heights. "I seek the monument of Thandbar," I said. "Can you tell me where to find it?"

"You think unshifterish," she commented, "when you ask where in Schlaizy Noithn you would find the monument of Thandbar."

I thought on this. It made a certain kind of sense. Thandbar had been the first and greatest of Shifters. Surely his memorial would not be a stable, unchanging thing. It would change, move, shift. "If you had to find it," I asked her, "where would you look?"

"Up and down, here and there, among, between, around, in and out of," she said.

"Upon," I offered. "Within, beneath, through and over . . ."

"Exactly," she replied. "That is more shifterish. There may be hope for Mavin's outland son."

5

Schlaizy Noithn

During the time that followed I learned of shifterish behavior, and thoughts, and habits. How could this be summed up so that you will understand, you of the world in which mountains do not walk and roadways do not run; you of the world in which you wake in the same place you have slept, find your way by landmarks, travel by maps and charts? Having made one journey in the little lake ship, I had seen, though learned nothing of the art of, guidance by the stars. In Schlaizy Noithn, that is what I did, for nothing but the stars remained unchanging through the nights and days of travel. I despair of explaining ''shifterish'' to you except to say that it is difficult for one reared in a Schooltown. And yet, from what I learned later, that rearing had been a mercy my Mother had given me which many young Shifters would have been glad to receive. Well, there is no better way to tell it than to tell it, as Chance would have said. So I will tell.

I entered the country of Schlaizy Noithn with Sambeline walking beside me. I said something or other, and she replied, making a remark about Mavin being much respected there, and after a short silence I turned to say something to her but found a huge, shambling pombi walking beside me, its monstrous head swinging to and fro with each step, long tongue lolloped between fangs of curved ivory. I was too frightened to do anything. My first thought was that this beast had killed Sambeline and left her bleeding body somewhere behind us, but when the beast looked up at me abstractedly before leaving the path to climb a hollow tree, to which it clung with one great, clawed foot while dipping into the hollow with the other to suck the honey-dripping paw with every evidence of pleasure, I began to guess that pombi and Sambeline were one. When the pombi blurred, shifted, and flew away through the trees on wide wings of softest white, calling a two pitched ooo-ooo as it went, when the honey tree shook itself and moved away through the forest on roots suddenly as flexible as fingers, leaving me alone, then I began to know what shifterish meant. I began to understand why it was that Sambeline had sneered at my belongings. Does a pombi need a blanket? A cookpot? A firestarter? I put down the pack and stared at it, unwilling to leave it and yet sure it marked me as nothing else could—stranger, outsider, outlander. Was this dangerous or otherwise? I could not tell.

Among the Gamesmen of Barish there were sixteen tiny figures representing Shifters. In an ordinary set of Gamesmen, such as are given to children for their little two-space games, these would be the pawns. In my set, Shifters; and one of them, or perhaps all of them held the persona of Thandbar, old sent-far himself, shiftiest of all. Presumably none of this would have been strange to *him*, and yet I never thought of taking a Shifter figure into my hand, never considered it. Later I wondered why I had not done. It was simple enough: pride. Shifting was my own talent, the one to which I had been born. I wanted no instruction in it from another. I wanted it to be mine. So, out of ignorance and pride, all unprepared for what I would meet or see or be required to do, I went on into the country of Schlaizy Noithn quite alone.

So.

I sat upon a hill beside a grotesque pile of stones, twisted and warped as though shaped thus when molten, making an uneasy meal of fish. These were unusual fish in that they had not howled and climbed up the fish spear to engulf my hands with a maw of ravening fury before melting into a swarm of butterflies and scattering into impalpability against the sky. Because these fish were quiet, these fish, reason said, were real fish, edible fish. Reason said that. Stomach was uncertain.

Beside me the warped stones grated into speech, moving slowly as lips might if they were as wide and tall as a man.

"Whoooo suuuups in Schlaaaaaizeee Noiiiiithnnnn?"

I said, "Peter, the son of Mavin Manyshaped," while trying to keep my heart from leaping out of my breast. The stone said nothing more. However, a long spit of earth began to grow from beside me, upward and outward like a curving branch of the living hill, out to turn again and look at me, opening from its tip a curious eye of milky blue, lashed with grasses, which blinked, blinked, blinked at me, staring. It stared while the fish cooked, while I ate them, while I scrubbed my knife and put it away, while I put out the fire, then turned to stare after me still as I walked away. When I looked back at the crest of the next hill, the eye had grown a bit taller to keep me in view.

Sometimes the road moved. Sometimes it moved in the direction I was going, sometimes sideways, sometimes backwards. Sometimes it jumped, like a cranky horse hopping when it is first saddled. When the road went against my direction, I got off as soon as possible, always apologizing for doing so—or for having been on it in the first place. It was hard to walk unless there was a road, for the land was full of impassable tangles. Sometimes the roads spoke to me, sometimes they cursed me. Once a road held fast to my feet while it carried me back a full day's journey. Will you understand my stupidity when I tell you that I walked the day's journey again on my own two feet, carrying my pack?

They—whoever they were—grew impatient.

I stopped when it grew dark, took my firelighter out of the pack and laid kindling beneath it, ready for the spark. The kindling reached up and flipped it out of my hands to be caught by a bird sitting on a stone. The bird flew away, carrying the firelighter in her claws, and I seemed to hear small, cawing laughter from the air. I cursed, cursed the place, the inhabitants, myself. Nothing seemed to hear me or care, save that the tops of the trees moved in a wind I had not felt till then and clouds began to boil in the sunset, so many puffy gray dumplings in a red soup of sky. Within moments it began to rain. My kindling grew legs and walked into the brush. I rolled myself into my blankets and nibbled on a handful of nuts collected during the day's travel. A stag came out of the forest, trumpeted challenge to another which appeared from behind me; the two charged one another over my body. I rolled, frantic, scraped across stones which left me bleeding, sat up to see the two stags running into the trees, my blankets caught upon their antlers.

I sat beneath a tree, water dripping down my neck, without blankets, without fire, the rain continuing in an endless, mocking stream. Whenever I moved, it found me. There was no shelter near except a hollow high in the tree into which wings flickered from time to time, outlined against flashes of lightning. I was cold. My clothes were little use except to hold some warmth against my body. I felt a little tug at one ankle. The next lightning flash showed a small, razor edged vine cutting the seams of my trousers while a tendril sifted a kind of powder on my boots. Two lightning flashes later and the boots were sprouting fungus from every surface, huge, soggy sponges covering my feet. Wings flickered into the hollow five manheights above me, an opening as wide as my armspan into the great tree.

A kind of dull fury began to pound in me, a discomfort so great that my body rebelled against it. There was no thought connected to it at all. Something deeper and more ancient than thought did as it wished, and Peter did nothing to oppose it.

My claws struck deep into the corky bark of the tree. My long, curved fangs gleamed in the lightning. Above me was a consternation of birds, and my pombi-self smiled in anticipation. I came through the opening into the hollow in a rush, a crunch of jaws, a flap of great paws catching this and that flutterer, to make a leisurely meal of warm flesh as I spat feathers out of the opening and watched the storm move away across the far hills. When it was quiet, I curled into the dry hollow, pausing only to rip out a strip of rotted wood which made a small discomfort against my hide. I slept. It was warm within the tree, and the fury passed as the storm passed.

I woke remembering this dimly, in my own body shape, naked as an egg. Below me the remains of my pack lay on the ground. A few straps and buckles. A knife. Beside me in the hole was the pouch in which the Gamesmen of Barish were stored. Evidently even in fury I had not let them go. I went down the tree as I had come up it, pombi-style, the pouch between my teeth. Once on the ground, however, I became Peter once more, furred-Peter, with a pocket in the fur to hold the

Gamesmen. It was no great matter. I wondered then, as I have since, why it took so long to think of it or decide to do it. The knife would have fitted into the pocket as well, but I left it where it lay. The pombi claws would cut as well.

As the sun rose higher and warmer, my fur grew shorter except upon the legs and feet where it was needed as protection against the stones and briars. When it grew cool with evening, the fur became long again. The body did it. Peter did not need to think of it. The body thought of longer legs on occasion, as well, and of arms which were variably long to pick whatever fruits were ripe. That day I ate better than in many days past. No fruit tore itself screaming from my hands. No fish or bird turned into a monster over my fire. Some things I let alone, and the body knew which. After a time, the eyes knew, also, and then the brain.

There were trees one did not approach, hills one stayed away from, roads one did not step upon. There were others which were hospitable, or merely "real." There were artifacts in Schlaizy Noithn. Monuments. Cenotaphs. Monstrous menhirs which looked as though they had been erected in the dawn of time. Some had been put there by—people. Gamesmen, perhaps. Or pawns. Some were Shifters, beings like myself (or so I thought) in the act of creation. I learned to trust the body's feeling about these places. If they were "real" then I might explore or take shelter there. If they were not, it were far better to stay a comfortable distance away. I did not yet know of other kinds of things, neither real nor Shifter, kinds of things my body would not warn me of. What betrayed me to one of these was simply loneliness.

Days had gone by. I had lost count of them. I had quartered the valley in search of the monument of Thandbar. I had searched and had begun to despair, for who was to say the monument had not moved always before me, or behind me? I had not seen a human form since Sambeline had flown away. I had wondered from time to time whether they used the human form only on some ceremonial occasions for some purpose of high ritual in the pursuance of their religion, whatever that might be. In any case, they did not show human form to me. I saw animals which were not animals, things apparently of stone and earth which were not, trees and plants which never sprouted from seed or tuber, but I did not see mankind. Even furred-Peter was far closer to his reality than many others there.

So, when I came upon the Castle, lit from a hundred windows, with a soft breath of music stirring from it into the airs of the night, I was needful more than I could say of that refreshment which comes from one's own kind. I was growing unsure of who I was, what I was. Was I only furred-Peter, running wild in the wilderness, an animal among others, gradually forgetting why I had come and to what end? I needed to be more than that.

So it called me where it stood upon its hill, brooding there over the silvered meadows, its great ornamental pillars contorted into bulbous asymmetries, casting lakes of shadow onto the grasses before me, making swamps of darkness within its courts. Its doors were open, welcoming. There was no warning. It was grotesque, misshapen, abnormal, but not fearsome. I was too lonely to be fearful. I shifted into a more civilized form, relishing the feel of clothing again, the weight of a cloak upon my shoulders. I had learned that clothing was no problem. One simply made it of the same stuff one used to make one's skin.

I walked under the arch, hands empty to show I was no enemy. Here was no portcullis to grind gratingly into stone pockets, no bridge to fall thunderingly upon the pavement. No, only an open way, the floor a mosaic design which swirled and warped, leading away in unexpected directions, returning from unexpected shifts and erratic lines. Looking at it made my head swim, but I told myself it was hunger for talk, for people, for a fire, for food that was cooked, for the trappings of humanity. The name of the place was carved over the great door. "Castle Lament." Well, A name without cheer, but not for that reason damnable. I had been in other places with sad names.

The door swung wider before me, and I went through.

Then it shut behind me.

How can I describe that sound? The door was not huge, no larger than in many great halls. It shut softly but with the *sound* of a door twenty times its size, a monstrous slam as of a mighty hammer, slightly clamoring, briefly echoing, fading into a silence which still reverberated with that sound, and all down the monstrous bulk of that place came the sound of other doors shutting with an equal finality, an inevitable shutting which I could not have imagined until that moment. I was shut in. I turned to beat my hands against the door, then stopped, afraid of what might come in answer to that knocking, for the sound of closing had been like jaws snapping shut, like hands clapping around fluttering wings, to hold, and hold, and hold until hope went, and life. It was the sound teeth might make, fastening in a throat.

I was terribly afraid, so afraid that I did nothing for a long moment, scarcely breathed, crouched where I was, peering into the place, seeing it as in a nightmare. At last I moved.

There were stairs which climbed from the audience hall over bottomless pits of black, arching against pillars to coil, snakelike, about them and climb upward to high pavements littered with a thousand half carven heads of stone which smiled at me and begged me in the voices of children for food, for the light of the sun, for escape. They rolled after me as I walked among them, pleading. I slipped through a door and shut it against their clamor, against the insistent knocking of the stone heads against the door.

There were roofless rooms with walls which seemed to go forever upward into darkness and at the top of that darkness the sound of something poised enormously and rocking, rocking, rocking. There were prodigious arches, windows leading into enclosed gardens in which stone beasts looked at me from wild eyes as though they wanted desperately to move. There were great halls in which fires burned and tables were set with steaming foods. I did not eat. I did not drink. But Shattnir within me drew the heat of those fires and stored it.

When I could go no further, it was beside one of the incredible hearths that I sat, hunkered upon a carpet woven with patterns of serpents and quadrumanna in intricate chase and capture. Shattnir drew power, and drew, and drew. Half sleeping, I let her draw, let her make me one great vessel of power. Far off through the halls of that place I could hear sounds once more, as of doors softly opening and closing, and I was afraid of what might be coming. My hand went into the pocket at my side. "Come, Grandmother," I whispered. "Divine Didir, come. . . ."

What came in answer to that clutching invitation was old, so old that my mouth turned dry and my skin felt crumbled and dusty. Ages settled on me, a thousand years or more. It was only a skin, a shriveled shell. There was nothing there, nothing—and then the skin began to fill, drawing from me, from Shattnir, from the world around us, began to swell, to grow, to push me from within until I thought there would be no place left for me to stand, and I cried in panic, "Stay, stay. Leave me room!" Then there came a cessation, a withdrawing, and a voice which whispered out of ancient years, "I see, I see, I see. . . ."

I sensed Dorn within, and Dorn's awe; Tràndilar, bowing down; Wafnor, head up, smiling; Shattnir offering her hand to that One I had raised from the ages. Grandmother Didir, Demon, First of all Gamesmen of the dim past, She who could Read the mind of this place, this monstrous place, if She would. If I had known the awe those others would feel, I would not have had the effrontery to raise Her up. I am glad, now, that I did not know. My other inhabitants had not been ignorant of my fear, now She was not ignorant of it. I heard all their voices, hers rising above them like a whisper of steel, infinitely fine, infinitely strong.

"Well, child. You have found a dangerous place."

"Sorcerer's Power Nine," whispered Shattnir.

"Necromancer Nine," said Dorn.

"Nonsense," she said. "Dangerous, not deadly. We old ones do not easily admit to 'deadly,' do we, child?"

I did not move, for she was reaching out from me, using the power Shattnir had gathered, reaching out through the very fabric of that labyrinthine construction to find its center, its mind. I felt the search go on and on, felt the blank incomprehension of the mighty walls, the stony ignorance of the pillars and stairs while she still searched, outward and outward from me to the very edges of the place. Nothing.

Down the corridor, a door opened.

"Below," she whispered, sending that seeking thought out and down, through mosaic floors and damp vaults, down to bottomless dungeons and endless catacombs which stretched beyond the walls away into lost silences. Nothing.

The door shut.

It seemed to me that I could hear Didir grit her teeth, a tiny grinding itch in my brain. "Up," and the mind went once more, more slowly, painstakingly, sifting each volume of air, each rising stair, climbing as the structure climbed into the lowering sky, wrapping each rising tower as a vine might wrap it, penetrating it with tiny thoughts like rootlet feet, to the summit of it all, the wide and vacant roofs. Nothing.

Just outside the room in which we were, not twenty paces down that great corridor, we heard a door open, heard the waiting pause, then heard it shut once more with that great, muffled sound as of an explosion heard at a distance. Oh, Lords of all Creation, we stirred in fear. Those within me gave shouted warning, but I needed none of them. I *flowed* up the wall, calling upon the power Shattnir had stored, flowed like climbing water, until I lay upon that wall no thicker than a fingernail, stretched fine and thin and transparent as glass, seeing through my skin, feeling through my skin, knowing and hearing with every fiber as the door into the room opened and something came through. The door shut once more.

But within the room something hissed, something ancient and malevolent. I could feel it, sense it, knew that it was there, but it was not there to any known sense of seeing. Protogenic and invisible, it filled the room, pressed against the walls, pressed against me in a fury of ownership of that space, that structure. Then slowly, infinitely slowly, without relinquishing any of the threatening quality, a door at the far side of the room opened and that which had inhabited the room flowed away. Behind it the door shut with that absolute finality I had heard over and over again.

"It knew someone was here," whispered Didir within. "But it did not know where you were."

I slid down the wall to lie in a puddle at its base, a puddle in which the little pouch which held the Gamesmen of Barish seemed the only solid thing. "Pull yourself together, boy," said Didir sternly. "Give me a shape I can think in!" She slapped at me, a quiver of electric pain which cared nothing for the shape I was in. I struggled into the form of furred-Peter, placed the Gamesmen in my pocket and waited. Far off and receding came the clamor of the great doors.

I eavesdropped then upon a conversation among ghosts. Dorn and Didir, Wafnor and Shattnir, with Trandilar as an interested observer, all talking at once, or trying to, as I tried to stay out of my own head enough to give them room. It went on for a long time, too long, for down the echoing corridors the sounds of the doors returned.

"Enough," I snapped, patience worn thin. "None of you is listening to the others. Be still. Let me have the use of my head!" There was a surprised silence and a sense almost of withdrawal, perhaps amused withdrawal. I didn't care. Let them laugh at me as they would. It was my body I needed to protect.

I set out my findings as Gamesmaster Gervaise had once taught me, high in the cold aeries of Schooltown, setting out the known, the extrapolated, the merely guessed. "Didir finds no mind in this place. If there were a mind, Didir would find it, therefore, there is no mind here. Nonetheless, we are in a place which shows evidence of intelligence, of design, a place which probably did not occur by accident or out of confusion. Therefore, if there is no mind now, at one time there was. If it is not here, it is gone—or elsewhere." I waited to be contradicted, but those within kept silent.

I went on obstinately, "Despite all this, there is something in the place, something primordial and evil, which allows outsiders to come in but will not let them out again. It is a trap, a mindless trap, inhabited by what?"

"A devil?" The voice was Wafnor's, doubtful.

"What are devils?" asked Didir.

Silence.

"What is left when the mind dies?" This was Dorn, thoughtful. "If the body were to go on living, after the mind were dead. . . ."

I thought. Beneath Bannerwell, in the dungeons there, after the great battle, we had found several Gamesmen with living bodies whom Silkhands the Healer had cried over, saying they should be allowed to die for their minds were already dead, root-Read, burned out, leaving only what she called living meat. They had breathed, swallowed, stared with sightless eyes at nothing. Himaggery had let her have her way, and she had sent them into kind sleep. Didir read my memory of this.

"What mind does the lizard have upon the rock?" she asked. "What mind the crocodilian in the mire? Mind enough to eat, to breathe, to fight, to hold its own territory against others of its kind—of any kind. So much, no more. No reason, no imagination. . . ."

"How long," breathed Dorn. "How long could it survive?"

"Forever," whispered Didir. "Why not? What enemies could stand against it?"

"So," I questioned them, "the creator of this place is . . . dead? Perhaps long dead? But something of . . . it . . . survives, some ancient, very primitive part?" Outside the room the hissing began, the door began to open. I flowed across the wall once more, quickly, for *it* entered the room in one hideous rush of fury. I sensed *something* which sought the intruder, *something* ready to rend and tear. This time it stayed within the room for a long, restless time, turning again and again to examine the room, the surfaces of it, the smell and taste of it. Terrified time passed until at last it flowed away again, out the other door, away down the corridors of the place.

"How do we stop it?" They did not answer me. "Come," I demanded. "Help me think! Was the place built? Or is it rather like that hillside I sat upon which spoke to me? Are we within the body of a Shifter?"

"It doesn't matter," said Wafnor. "Call upon my ancestor, Hafnor, the Elator, who is among the Gamesmen. Call upon him and we will be transported from this place. . . ."

I gritted my teeth at the temptation. "Had I desired that, I would have called him rather than Grandmother Didir. Think of the stone heads. The beasts in the gardens. Shall we leave them here forever to cry out their pain?" This was presumptuous of me, but I had resolved that no cry for help would find me wanting in the future. The fate of Himaggery and Windlow—and, perhaps, Izia—burned too deep within me, the guilt too fresh to allow another yet fresher. I felt them move within me, uneasily, and it made me feel dizzy and weak, depleted of power.

"Ah, well," said Wafnor from within. "If we cannot find the mind, then we must attack the body."

I felt him reaching out with his arms of force, out and out to a far, slender tower upon the boundary of the building, felt him push at it using all the power Shattnir had built up for him. The tower swayed, rocked, began to fall. From somewhere in that vast bulk came a screaming hiss, a horrid cacophony of furious sound, a drum roll of doors opening and closing down the long corridors toward that tower. Like a whip, Wafnor's power came back to us, reached once more, this time in the opposite direction. He found a curtain wall over a precipice and began to hollow the earth from beneath it, swiftly, letting the stone and soil tumble downward as the bottom layers weakened. I felt the wall begin to go, slowly, leaning outward in one vast sheet which cracked and shattered onto the stones far below. Within the castle the sound of fury redoubled, a rushing of wind went through the place from end to end, seeking us, searching for us. The hissing grew to a roar, a frenzied tumult.

"The thing is hurt," said Didir. "See the doors. . . ."

Indeed, the doors stood open into the corridor, open here and there up and down that corridor, moving as though in a wind, uncertain whether to open further or close tight. Wafnor reached out once more, this time to a point of the wall midway between his two former assaults, once more undermining the wall to let it shatter onto the mosaic paving in a thunder of broken stone. The door before us began to bang, again and again, a cannonade of sound. Between one bang and the next came a long, rumbling roar, and the stone heads burst through the open door to ricochet from wall to wall, side to side, screaming, eyes open, stone lips pouring forth guttural agonies. The clamor increased, and they rolled away, still shrieking, as Wafnor began to work on the fourth side of the castle. The walls of the room began to buckle.

"It is striking at itself," whispered Didir. I pulled myself across the room, onto the opposite wall, watching and listening with every fiber. The wall opposite me breathed inward, bulging, broke into fragments upon the floor and through it into the endless halls below. Then Wafnor came back to me, and we did not move, did not need to move, for around us Castle Lament pursued its angry self-destruction, biting at itself, striking at itself in suicidal frenzy. Walls crumbled, ceilings fell, great beams cracked in two to thrust shattered ends at the sky like broken bones. Then, suddenly, beam and stone and plaster began to fade, to blur, to stink with the stink of corruption. Gouts of putrescence fell upon us, rottenness boiled around us. I rolled into myself, made a shell, floated upon that corruption like a nut, waited, heard the scream of that which died with Castle Lament fade into silence, gone, gone.

When the silence was broken by the songs of birds, I unrolled myself into furred-Peter once more. I stood upon a blasted hill, upon a soil of ash and cinder, gray and hard, upon which nothing grew. Here and there one stone stood upon another, wrenched and shattered, like skeletal remains. Elsewhere nothing, nothing except the stone heads, the stone beasts, silent now, with dead eyes. I kicked at one of them and it fell into powder to reveal the skull within. It, too, stared at me with vacant sockets, and I wept. "Shhh," said Didir within. "It does not suffer."

At the foot of the hill, two trees shivered and became two persons, youths, fair-haired and solemn. A pombi walked from the forest, stood upon its hind legs and became Sambeline. A bird roosted upon one of the stone heads, crossed its legs and leaned head upon hand to look at me with the eyes of a middle-aged man. Slowly they assembled, some of the Shifters of Schlaizy Noithn, to stare at me and at the ruins, curiously—and curiously unmoved.

At length I looked up and demanded of them, "How long was this place here?"

The bird man cocked his head, mused, said, "Some thousand years, I have heard."

"What was it? It was a Shifter, wasn't it?"

"I have heard it was one called Thadigor. He was mad. Quite mad."

"He was not mad." I forced them to meet my eyes. "He was dead."

"That could not be," said Sambeline. "If he had been dead, Castle Lament would have gone. . . ."

"No," I swore at them all. "The Shifter was dead. His mind had died long ago. Only some vestige of the body remained, some primitive, compulsive nerve center which kept things ticking over, the fires lit, the walls mended, doors opening and closing, holding and hating. Only that." I waited, but they said nothing. "How many of you has it taken . . . captured . . . killed?"

"Few . . . of us," said the bird man.

"Ah. So you warned your own? But you let others learn for themselves. Or die for themselves. How many went in?"

"Thousands," said Sambeline moodily.

"And how many came out?"

"None," said the bird man.

"Wrong," I said. "They have all come out. All. And now, I demand of you an answer which I have earned from you. Where is the monument of Thandbar?"

They looked at one another, shifty looks, gazes which glanced away from eyes and over shoulders to focus on distant things.

"I can do to others what I did to Castle Lament," I threatened, softly. "No matter what shape you take, I will find you. . . ."

It was Sambeline who spoke, placatingly. "Schlaizy Noithn is the monument to Thandbar," she said. "All of it. The whole valley."

Almost I laughed. Oh, Mavin, I thought. Mother, are you of this shifty kindred, this collection of lick-spittle do-nothings? And, if so, do I want to find you at all? My eyes went to the heights. "Look not upon it," she had written. Well, if I look not upon Schlaizy Noithn, I would look upon the heights. Somewhere up there.

I did not speak to those who still stood in the wreckage. I turned from them all and went away toward the heights. Behind me I heard voices raised briefly in argument. When I looked down from the trail they had gone. The valley was as I had seen it first, green, wooded, garlanded with rivers and jeweled with lakes. At the edge of the valley nearest me was a scar of gray. "Become grass, and cover it," I whispered to them. "To hide your shame." Within me, Didir stirred. "Never mind," I said. Let them look upon the scarred earth for a while. Perhaps it would make them think of something they should have done. Or

would have done, had they learned any of the words old
Windlow taught me.

In that moment I would not have given a worm-eaten fruit for
all the Shifters in Schlaizy Noithn.

6

Mavin's Seat

At the top of the slope a trail led around the valley. I turned toward the west since this was the direction opposite the one from which I had come into Schlaizy Noithn. The way led higher and higher, ending at last at a pinnacle which speared out westward over the lands beyond. I leaned against a tree, staring at the far horizons from ice-topped mountains in the south to a far, mist-shrouded land in the north where the jungly swamps were to be found. I leaned, thinking of nothing much, until a movement caught my eye. There upon the pinnacle was Mavin, crouched above a fire over which several plump birds were roasting. My mouth filled so in anticipation of the taste of them that I could not speak as I approached.

She looked up at me and snarled, "What kept you? I expected you long since."

It was too much. I felt the hot fury build in me and blow up my backbone like a hard wind. "How could you allow an abomination like that to exist?" I screamed at her. "Centuries of it. Festering like a sore! And you did nothing. Nothing! I came close to being killed. Like the thousands who were killed! Who were they? Little people? Pawns? People of no consequence? Eaten up in play? How could you let your own flesh fall into that trap? How could you . . . ." I sputtered out, made mute by rage.

She did not seem to have listened. She plopped one of the birds upon a wooden trencher, dumped a spoonful of something else at its side, added a hunk of bread and set it all on a stone beside me. "You'll be hungry," she said. "Exorcism is hard work."

82

I screamed at her again. She bit neatly into a leg of fowl, using one finger to tuck in a bit of crispy skin. The smell ravished me. She said, "Your dinner will get cold."

I raged, howled, strode back and forth in a perfect frenzy of extemporaneous eloquence. She went on eating. At last the exertion of the day, the long rage, and sheer weariness caught up with me. I choked, gagging on my own words. At this, she put a wooden mug into my hand. I thought it was water, drank half of it in a gulp, then choked myself into silence. It was pure spirit of wine, wineghost, and it burned away my fury, sweeping through me like a broom through a midden. "Allllg," I said. "Allllg."

"Exactly." She placed the trencher in my hands. "If you have done with your peroration, my son, I will answer your charges. How old do you think I am? No. Never mind. Surely you do not think me a thousand years old? No. I thought not. Well, then, I can disclaim any responsibility for that place you speak of for at least nine hundred years. Since I became aware of it as a curse upon the valley of Schlaizy Noithn, I have tried three times to correct the matter. I tried first to get some of those stiff-necked Immutables to come into the valley. I was sure the Shifter was mad, and I told the Immutables so, but they would not come. None of their affair, they said, whether it ate a thousand Gamesmen or a thousand thousand. Later, I tried to get a noted Healer to come with me into the valley. He refused me, saying he felt the chance of success was small. My third attempt succeeded. Castle Lament is gone, and you are here, eating roast fowl and none the worse for it."

I stared at her, unbelieving. She had meant me to fall into that . . . that . . .

"I was right, wasn't I?" she asked. "It was mad?"

"It was dead," I mumbled. "Dead, and I could've been killed. . . ."

"Nonsense. You are my son. You are a Shifter. Shifters of Mavin's line do not 'get killed.' We are too shifty, too clever, too sly. . . . Besides, you have help."

The wineghost had seeped into my fingers and toes, warming and tickling them into a feeling almost of comfort. The food slid down my throat. I could not summon the energy for anger. "You got me drunk," I accused.

"I know how to deal with hysteria," she said stiffly. "You did take your time in coming to visit me. Did the invitation confuse you?"

"No . . . no. I wanted to come. But others wanted me to stay. Time went by."

"The journey? Was it easy?"

"The worst was the Trader. I did think I might be killed there. He tried. . . ."

"Nap? A smallish man with a wide mouth? Mouth all full of smiles and easy words? Eyes full of flint and old ice? That one?"

I nodded yes. "Stupid. I was stupid to fall in with him. But he was persistent. . . ."

"He is that." Her voice grated.

"It took me a while to figure out he wanted to kill me. Or something else. I'm not really sure."

"What did he try?"

"Drugged wine. Or poisoned. No, I think drugged, because he was wild when I convinced him I was dead." I went on to tell her in fits and starts what had occurred during the journey, leaving out nothing except what had set me off in haste to her in the first place. Well, I was full of wineghost. When I told her of my long trials in Schlaizy Noithn, she shook her head.

"We call it the monument of Thandbar, true. Howsomever, it is as much a nursery as anything else. Many of those there are new come to their Talents, or very young, or limited. Sambeline has only three shapes, her own, a pombi, and an owl. Many there are were-owls or were-pombis. Some there are experimentalists, madmen or women who cannot adapt to the Talent at all, who shift and become locked into strangeness. Roads which move. Speaking hillocks. Some experiment themselves into shapes they cannot get out of. I think Castle Lament was one such. I have long thought it would be worthwhile to have a few Immutables available to unlock them, but I have been unable to convince the Immutables of that."

"They have no fondness for Gamesmen." I yawned. "Though Riddle has been very kind to me."

"Well, perhaps we can call upon that kindness come someday. Tell me of my kindred? Is Mertyn well? Does he plot still with Himaggery and old Windlow?"

I cursed myself. She didn't know. I had sat by her fire eating and drinking for an hour, and she did not know. I blurted it all out, the disappearances, Himaggery gone, Windlow gone, Mertyn in the Bright Demesne. She looked at me frozen-faced with suspicious wetness at the corner of one eye.

"Himaggery vanished! Oh, Gameslords, but I feared it would happen. He is a sweet man, full of juice as ripe fruit." She paused, and then said, "He is your father. I remember him kindly always, though he does not so remember me. He would have had me stay with him and live with him like some pawnish wife of a farrier; me, Mavin Manyshaped, for whom the world is not too large! So I left him against his will and he likes me no longer."

"Does he know? Did he . . . I mean, that he is my father?"

"Oh, knowing I am your mother and what your age is, he should have figured it out. Yes. I should think so. Not that it matters. Which is what I told him, but he was full of pawnish ideas. Enough. Whether he likes me well or not at all, still I would not have him vanished into the shadows like so many of our friends. Mertyn did well to send you to me. Now. What's to do about this. . . ."

"Mertyn wanted me to find them, search for them. He told me to ask for them wherever I went, as Necromancer. . . ."

"Tush. Those who are vanished in this way are not dead. We had figured that out a decade ago. Nor do they live, for the Pursuivants cannot find them. No, it is into the Land of Dingold they have gone, the place of shadows, and it is there we must Shift to find them. Nap, now, he knows something, you may be sure."

This abrupt change of subject caught me by surprise, and seeing this, she pointed down from the height we sat upon to the place below, slowly emerging into the light as the shadow of the precipice grew shorter. I peered down at strangeness, stranger even than Schlaizy Noithn, for it looked like nothing I had seen before that time, a weirdness lying below us at the foot of the cliff.

If a giant child had built a mud-spider out of shreds and threads, rat fur and murk, then set it upon a stone dish with its legs arrayed full circle around it and its eyes glittering in all directions, this might have been likened to what I saw. Then, if the child had built bulky mud towers between the spider's legs, each tower with doors at the bottom in the shape of faces, each face a maw opening into the dark—why then, that might have been likened to what I saw. Then, if the child had surrounded it all with a saw-edged wall and set the whole thing in quivering motion—well, that was the place. Smoke rose from it. Clangor sounded from it, soft with distance. The faces upon the tower doors grimaced, eyes first open then shut. The spider turned its eyes this way and that, the whole a clot, a bulk of dark in the light of morning.

"What is it?" I whispered, unbelieving.

"The Blot," she said. "To which Gifters come. Nap among them."

"Gifters!"

"Traders. They call themselves Traders. They are Gifters nonetheless. They bring certain things here, they take certain things from here. The things they take from here they sell, sometimes. Often they give."

"Is this—the place of magicians?"

"What do you know of magicians?" she demanded.

"Only what is said in the marketplace. What Gamesmaster Gervaise said. What Laggy Nap said. That there may be, perhaps, a place of magicians to the west. Gervaise says the little cold Gamespieces come from there. Nap says no such thing, but we both know he is a liar."

"Some call the place below there a place of magicians. But there are no Gamesmen there. No Immutables. Only a few very strange beings which stay there and other strange creatures which come and go. And soon now, Nap again. He comes regularly, and last time he came here, he left here with your cousins in his train."

"My cousins?" I remembered two grinning faces under flame-red hair, peering down at me from a height before the battle at Bannerwell. "My cousins? With Nap?"

"Your cousins. Swolwys and Dolwys. Twins. Scamps. But better Shifters than any you met in Schlaizy Noithn. They have not your advantages, no Gamesmen of Barish to call upon (as I presume you did in Castle Lament, as I intended) but good boys for all that. I sent them to join Nap's train the last time he came to the Blot, and I let them go and return by that road to the north.

If we had no other evidence, the fact that Nap travels *that* road would tell us what he is. Past Poffle. Too close. But they should return soon.''

She was staring away to the north where a pair of ruts wound around the edge of the plateau and disappeared. Following her gaze I could see a plume of dust there. Someone was upon that road, certainly, and it came in only the one direction, toward the place below.

''There they are. Still some hours away, coming no faster than the pace of their water oxen. So, if I were you, my son, I'd sleep a while. Drink the rest of your wineghost and take your full stomach into my cavern yonder. I will call you when they come.'' She gestured toward a half hidden entrance I had not noticed before. I was too weary to argue, so let her push me in that direction.

When I came to the cave entrance, I looked back expecting to see her still watching from the prominence, but it was bare. High above me circled a huge bird with wings as long as I am tall. It cried my name and dipped toward me, then caught a current of air to carry it north. It was very beautiful in the sun, white and gleaming, trailing plumes graceful as smoke. I went into the cave with a feeling of exquisite sadness, as though ridden by a memory I could not identify. Had I seen her so before? Or was it something in her voice as she cried to me? Perhaps it was only the spirit in my blood, the aftermath of anger. I was asleep as soon as I lay down.

She woke me in the late afternoon, shaking me and offering some warm brew from a simmering pot by the fire. ''They have stopped,'' she said. ''It is as though Nap is not eager to come to the Blot. They have come almost to the wall, however, and you can see them easily from the pinnacle.''

So I went onto the pinnacle once more to watch the compact circle of wagons near the cinereous walls. The animals were unhitched and led away to a patch of tall meadow grass near the bottom of the long slope. Mavin watched the animals with curious intensity. Until that moment I had given no thought as to what guise my cousins had taken in Nap's train. Now her focused gaze told me where they were and in what shape. A pair of oxen grazed away from the others, toward a stony place heavy with obscuring shadows, grazed around, behind them, and was gone. A rustle among small trees marked their passage.

"They will be here momentarily," she said with satisfaction. "Perhaps we may learn something. . . ." There was the sound of plodding on the trail, silence, and then they appeared around the high stone, precisely as I remembered them. Broad-faced, red-haired, with grins of the same width on lips of the same shape. One of them had an interesting scar over one eye. Otherwise they were identical. The scarred one pointed to his identifying mark.

"Swolwys," he said. "I keep the scar to make it easier for others to address me by name. It is easier than Shifting into something unique."

"Our similarity is uniqueness enough," said the other. "Why should we not be known for that fact as well as any other? I am Dolwys. Those mental midgets in the wagon train did not even notice that they had two identical water oxen. We did it to see if they were alert. They are not, or at least, not very. They even believed you dead, Cousin Peter."

I swallowed. They looked very young to be so insouciant, younger even than I. "I take it you were not convinced."

Swolwys considered this. "Ah, had we not known who and what you are, it is possible we would have been taken in. It was very well done. Except that we could not figure out why you did not simply Shift and slide away."

"There was a woman in the train," I said.

"Ah," said Dolwys. "Izia."

"Lovely Izia," commented his twin. "Not a type attractive to me, but still, fair. Very fair."

Mavin's head had come up like a questing fustigar's. "A woman? What is she to you?"

"She is nothing to me." I laughed, somewhat bitterly. "Why this concern? She is a pawn, a servant. She is in durance, held unwillingly, captive by some device I have not seen or heard of before. Boots. Metal boots, high on the leg, which grow hot at Nap's will. Had I simply vanished, Nap might have thought the woman involved in my disappearance, for I had been stupid enough to let him see me watching her. As you say, she is very fair."

"But she is nothing to you?"

I began to bridle at this repeated question. "Not quite nothing, no! She is a captive. As were those in Castle Lament. I have told you my feelings about such matters.''

"Ah. Well. Perhaps we can do something about it."

At that moment, I was glad there was no Demon among them. I had not been able to say she was nothing to me with an honest heart. She was a good deal to me, and the fact that she was now almost within reach of my voice made me tremble. Izia. I could not leave her to Nap's malevolence. I would have to find a way to free her. I did not understand the compulsion, for it was not merely pity, but I welcomed it as I now supposed I had welcomed Sylbie and Castle Lament. They were all problems, problems to be solved, wrongs to be righted. I thought again of Windlow's curious word: Justice. It was odd how many satisfying things could be done under that rubric. So, I ruminated while my cousins and mother leaned upon the stone to watch the wagons below.

"There," whispered Mavin. "Nap has decided to wait until morning to enter the Blot." It was true. The camp had settled; Nap was seated beside his fire as others moved about the endless duties of the train. I saw Izia at once, moving among the animals, searching for the missing pair, her skirted figure plain among the trousered ones of the men, all walking with that strange hesitation which I now, too well, understood.

"Is there some way we can free them?" I asked the twins. "From Nap, or from the boots?"

"If it becomes important, we must find a way," said Swolwys. "However, those boots are locked on in a way we do not understand. I have heard Nap say that an Elator in those boots could not move out of them. A Tragamor could not move them from himself. A Shifter could not change out of them. They transcend Talent, so says Nap. Nap controls them, but he must return to the Blot every season to have that power renewed. It is growing weaker even now, and I think it is only that which brings him back to the Blot. Without his power, control of his servants wanes. The last day or two we have seen indications of rebellion among the pawns, particularly the newest ones. We went far to the south, you know, looking for you, I suppose, cousin. We stopped near the Bright Demesne. You were not there, but Nap bought pawns from a pawner, young, strong ones who look at him with mutiny in their eyes.''

"Izia? Is she likely to mutiny?"

"No. Nap has had her since she was a child. He taunts her with that fact. He tells her that she was sold to him by a Shifter because she was worthless, that only Nap's kindness and forbearance have kept her alive these years. He has had her in the boots since she was seven or eight years old, for ten years, at least. Those years have bent her. She does not mutiny. She scarcely lives."

"Why does he hold her so? Why?"

The twins gave me a curious look, and Mavin speared me with one of her imperious stares, but Swolwys replied readily enough. "She comes of a line of horsebreeders and farriers from the South. Skill with animals is bred into that line as Talent is with us. She can do anything with horses, with almost any animal, and she is worth a thousand times her price to Nap. Also, she is fair. . . ."

I did not want to hear about that. The thought of her in Nap's sleazy embrace was more than I could bear. "What now?" I asked.

"Now you will take Swolwys' place," said Mavin. "You will go down to Nap's camp. We need to know what happens inside those walls on the morrow." She gave me another look, daring me to disagree, but I had no thought of that. No, I would have begged to go. I needed to see that Izia still lived . . . as I remembered her.

7

The Blot

I was accepted among the water oxen as a water ox, that is, after I had laid hands upon the real beast enough to know how one was made. I had already learned it was easier to become something entirely imaginary than to become something which had a recognized form and movement of its own. Thus, for the first few hours of wateroxship, it was necessary to admonish myself to keep my head down, my tail in motion against the flies, my floppy feet out from under one another. Being a fustigar had been easier for me, once, but then I had seen fustigars every day of my life. Water oxen were more rural animals, certainly smellier ones. Dolwys whispered to me that I could stop monitoring my own behavior when the smell no longer seemed foreign. It did not take as long as I had expected.

I learned in the transformation to pick up bulk, a thing I had not known before. At first inert, as one maintained a form the excess bulk became incorporated gradually into the flesh of the creature. When one shifted back, there was a certain bulk left over. Some Shifters, as the hillock had in Schlaizy Noithn, simply gained and gained until that network of fibers which made Shifters what they were was stretched so far it could not assume its original form. It was all in this network, so Mavin said. She had already harvested the flesh left over when Dolwys and Swolwys had Shifted back into human form. It was too scattered to make chops, she said, but it would make good soup. I confess a certain queasiness about this. I did not like the thought of eating what had once been a part of my cousins. They laughed at me when I said this, making me feel very young and foolish. Nonetheless, I did not like the idea and was glad it was not put to the test. Instead of soup, I learned to eat grass.

I learned that Shifters had a jargon of their own, almost a language. Changing back into an original form was called "pulling the net," evidently from that network of fibers which transferred more or less intact from creature to creature, from form to form. One could "be" a bird with only about half the network. One could "be" a water ox with about two-thirds of it. What was left over simply lay about inside, doing nothing, available to "become" other things, clothing or whatever. It was all very interesting.

At any rate, by morning I was an unremarkable water ox, driven from my graze to a wagon and hitched there, able to see Izia whenever I swung my head in her direction. Laggy Nap had at last decided to go the final few paces of his journey, into the shadowy courts of the Blot. The gates were open when we approached. They looked as though they had been open for a generation or more, hinges rusted and hanging, metal doors bent and sagging, grass pushing up between the stones. Inside the gates the shadows of the huge, spidery arches fell upon us, and a Tower-face mumbled at us from across the pavement. Dolwys whiffled as though startled, and I remembered that I was a water ox which would have been startled at such a sight and whiffled with him, hearing Izia's voice, "Shaaa, shaaa, shaa, still now, nothing to bother about, my strong ones. Shaaa, shaaa." The sound of her voice made me shiver involuntarily; perhaps any water ox would have shivered at it.

We saw the first inhabitant of the place as it came mincing across the pavement, and for a moment I thought I had not managed the Shift of my eyes properly. Something was monstrously wrong with the shape which confronted us, and it stood before us for some time before my mind believed what my eyes saw. This was no Shifter. It was a true-person, or perhaps two persons. From the waist up it was two, two heads, two sets of shoulders, four arms, two chests tapering into one waist, one set of hips and legs. It chortled, "Dupey one," out of one mouth as the other mouth said in a deeper voice, "Dupey two." I looked up to see Izia trembling upon her seat and Laggy Nap striding forward with every expression of confidence.

"Oyah, Dupies. Will you stable the beasts in the yard, or would you rather we stake them outside the walls?" His voice was ingratiating, a tone I had not heard him use except when he had sought to seduce me into his train outside Betand.

The tenor head answered, 'Oh, here, here, Laggy Nap, here. Where Dupies can watch them, feed them, brush their pretty hides. You let Dupies have them. We'll love them all to bits, nice things, great, wonderful beasties."

Beside me Dolwys trembled. I, too, at the lustful endearments which sounded to me much like hunger. The deeper voice said, 'Oh, see how it shivers, pretty beasty is cold, all cold from the shadow. Bring it in the sun, Dupey, where it is warm. . . ."

"Fine," said Nap heartily. "You take them along into the sun and bring them food and water, Dupies. They'll love you for that."

"Ooooh, love us all to bits, the big things will."

"Love us, yes they will." The two led us off, the one led us off, caroling their—its pleasure. Beside me Dolwys trembled again and again. I wondered what he was thinking. We were too much in evidence to talk. It would have to wait. We were taken to a sunny spot near a trough of water, and a cart of hay was pushed near to us. We swished our tails and swung our muzzles under the pattering hands and constant voices of the Dupies, trying to see through them or around them to what Nap and the others were doing.

"Where is Fatman? Dupies, where is Fatman?" Nap was persistent in the question, as he needed to be to draw the monster's attention away from us.

"Fatman? Oh, Fatman is here. Maybe in a little while, Laggy Nap. He was here a while ago. Patience, patience. He will be here."

"Tallman? Is Tallman here as well?"

"Oh, yes. Tallman is always here. Always sometimes. He goes and comes, Laggy Nap. Patience, patience." The two heads turned to one another, kissed passionately, hugged one another fiercely and went back to their patting and brushing of the horses. They had not groomed us yet. I found myself begging that they would not. This was not to be, however, and I was thoroughly fondled as was Dolwys at my side, with such hungry tenderness that we were both shaking by the time the

Dupies had made off and left us. At last we could watch the people of the train, but they might have been made of stone, slumped as they were on the shadowy pavement of the place near one of the great, mouthy doors. None moved except Nap, striding among them, slapping his hands along his thighs, clicking his heels upon the stone, toc, toc, toc, an erratic rhythm. From some hidey hole we could hear the Dupey voices calling, "Patience, patience, Laggy Nap."

The first evidence of other inhabitants came in a shrill, premonitory shrieking, like a tortured hinge crying stress into the quiet of the place. It came from within one of the towers, behind the mumble lips of the doors. The shriek became a rumble, the rumble a clatter and one of the mouths began to open, reluctantly, wider and wider until the eyes disappeared in wrinkles and the teeth gaped wide above a metal tongue extending outward, toward us. Down this ramp rolled a figure as strange in its way as the Dupies were in theirs, round, so fat that the shoulders bulged upward and the cheeks outward to make a single convex line which blended into a spherical form, a balloon, a ball, an egg of a man. He rode in a kind of cup, like an eggcup on wheels, and it was this vehicle which made the extraordinary shrieking noise.

"Oil, Dupies," it cried. "Oil for the Fatwagon. Oh, she screams, doesn't she. Makes a terrible racket. Laggy Nap, walla, wallo, holla hello, listen to me come screaming at you. Oil! Oil! Dupies!"

"Patience, patience, Fatman," came the answering call, evidently the standard reply to all happenings in this place. The Fatman rolled his eggcup backward and forward, sending all the animals into frenzies at the high-pitched sound, until the Dupies ran from whatever place they had been hiding. They bore a can of oil, and a kind of tag game ensued during which the sounds gradually diminished into almost quiet. It was only then that Laggy Nap came forward once more.

"I greet you, Fatman."

"Oh, I greet you as well, Laggy Nap. Have you a fine cargo for us this time? Something to please *them*? Something to make the great, tall things happy? I do hope so. They become difficult, Laggy Nap. Sensitive. Given to fits and hurling things at us for no reason. Oh, my, my, my, my, yes. They need distractions, Laggy Nap, indeed yes.''

"I have most of what I was sent for, yes.''

"Most? Do you say 'most,' Laggy Nap? Ah, to have only *most* may not be enough. It is far better to have *more*, not most. Well, he will be in a temper, you may be sure. Tallman will be in a temper, Laggy Nap. All the Tallmen. All. He'll tell you so, even if I don't.'' And the Fatwagon rolled away among the towering arches and the mumbling door-faces, exclaiming to itself as it went, careening here and there, light glistening again and again in the gloom from the bald pate of Fatman where he wheeled his way into the shadows.

I heard Izia say to Laggy Nap, "Why will you not let us go outside? We are no good to you here. Let us take the animals outside the walls. We will wait for you there." Her voice was hopeless, even as she begged.

"I want you here!" he hissed, fingers jumping along the seam of his trousers, tap tap, full of an energy and rhythm of their own. "Here."

"We sicken," she murmured. "All of us, animals, all. In here. In the gloom of this place, we cannot help it. We sicken."

"So, sicken. I care not whether you sicken. Sicken silently. I swear, I will find that Shifter who sold you to me and sell you back to him or have vengeance upon him for cheating me as he did."

"You were not cheated, Laggy Nap! I have driven your animals across this world a dozen times in the ten years you have had me. Who treats your team beasts when they are injured or ill? Who gets them across fords they will not cross and up trails they will not climb? Who but me, Laggy Nap? You were not cheated.''

"I say I was because you do not give me peace. Now be silent or burn a little." His fingers tapped a different rhythm, and she caught her breath in sudden pain.

I moved, and Dolwys immediately put one of his great, floppy feet upon mine, half tripping me in the process. I heard him sigh, "wait," or some such word, blown through his water ox throat. I subsided, frustrated, unable to do more than ache at her hurt. In any case, Nap did no more than twinge at her, perhaps because his powers were much dwindled and perhaps because the careening Fatwagon came barreling out of the dusk into our midst, its occupant caroling madly.

"Tallman's coming, Laggy Nap. I sent the call, just as I knew you'd want me to, and he's coming swiftly. Watch the big mouth, now, Laggy Nap, he's on his way. Come Dupies, come and watch. Tallman's coming."

The Dupies emerged from twilight places, chattering at one another like sparrows, patting at one another with their swift little hands, eyebrows cocked and mouths moving, all the time stroking at one another, pausing only to hug and kiss with that same greedy passion they had displayed toward the animals. They paused before one of the mumbling Tower mouths, waited in hushed expectancy. Reluctantly, Laggy Nap took up a position beside them and the Fatwagon rolled to one side. There was a long hush, then the sound of far off machinery in motion, a rumbling which vibrated the ground beneath us and sent all the Tower mouths into fits of grimaces.

The mouth before us turned downward, an introspective frown, followed by an expression of alertness, wonder, and then it opened to vomit out its own metal tongue, an endless tongue which extruded itself into a platform a little raised above the surface on which we stood. Onto this platform rolled a little car, somewhat like those I have seen used in some pawnish mines to transport ore, except this one was flat. From its prow there stuck up a tall beam, narrow and high. The beam broke itself into angles and stepped down from the car, its top section bending to look down upon us all.

"Tallman," cried the Dupies.

"Tallman," Fatman warbled in the same tone.

"Tallman," said Laggy Nap, his fingers jerking along the seams of his trousers. As for the rest of us, we animals, we pawns and animals, we said nothing but stared and stared. The voice, when it came, was a woodwind sound, a reed sound, deep and narrow-edged.

"Well, Laggy Nap. You have returned. Have you fulfilled the orders I gave you?"

Fumble, fumble, fingers tap tap along trouser seams, feet shuffle back and forth, pale as paper, Laggy Nap. "I have most of what I was sent for, Tallman. The youth, Peter—the Necromancer, he was killed on the journey. . . .''

A long, long pause during which that narrow, hooded head bent above Laggy Nap as some great serpent head might bend above its prey. ''Killed? How killed? By you?''

''No, Tallman! Never! It was a rockslide on the southern route, in the canyons there. He would go that way, and mindful of your orders, we went with him until we could be sure to take him without injuring him. He went to the canyon wall to relieve himself, Tallman, and the wall broke over him. More rock than the train could move in a season, Tallman. His body, under all that rock . . .'' Nap's voice faded into uncertainty, and the head above him never moved but brooded still in that unrelenting scrutiny.

''How long ago?''

''How long? Ah, let me think. We have been thirty-five days on the northern route, Izia, wasn't it thirty-five days? Then there was a space of three days getting back to Betand. Less than forty days, Tallman. Thirty-eight, I would say.''

''Not so long, then, that you could not take a Necromancer there and raise him. Raise this Peter. Find out from his spirit what it was he knew. Not too long for that?''

''Oh, I could do that. Yes.'' He gave a little hop, as though eager to be on his way. ''I need only to have my power renewed, Tallman. And to unload the cargo.''

There was a silence, a silence which drew out into a swamp of stillness in which no one moved. Laggy Nap himself did not seem to breathe. He might have forgotten how to breathe, so still he was, and when Tallman spoke at last the air came out of Nap as out of a balloon. ''No, Laggy Nap. No power renewal this time. We will give you power when you return.''

''But, but . . .'' Teeth chattering, face like melting ice. ''How will I keep the pawns in order? How keep the beasts in order, the work done? How keep Izia doing her work. . . .''

The impossibly tall figure straightened itself. ''You will leave the pawns here. *They* need some pawns. To make blueş. For a ceremony. You will leave the woman here. I need a woman for . . . something. You will take one wagon and go. And you will wear the boots to be sure you return.''

Fatman burbled, chortled, "Boots, Tallman. Whose boots for Laggy Nap? Does Tallman have extra boots he wishes to be used for Laggy Nap?"

And the Dupies, "Patience, patience, Laggy Nap. We will find boots for him. . . ."

Tallman growled something, beckoned to Izia where she crouched ashen-faced against a pillar. She sidled toward him fearfully, and he bent above her. "Take off the boots."

"They will not come off," she whispered, hysterical, panting.

"Fool! They would not come until now. They will come off now. Take them off."

So, she drew them from her legs almost before my eyes, and I could see what had happened to her legs from the years she had worn them, old scars and lines of festering red, a scaly peeling surface where there should have been maiden smoothness. She saw her own legs and crawled away, retching and gasping. Dolwys put his foot upon mine once more, and again I heard that same, sighed word. "Wait."

It was the Dupies who put the boots upon Laggy Nap, one of them holding him while the other drew them on. When it was done, Tallman tapped at his sides and Laggy Nap screamed.

"So," said the Tallman, "you will be able to feel my impatience even to the ends of the world, Laggy Nap. Now, unload your cargo and get you gone to do what I have ordered. Go to Betand. Find a Necromancer there. Promise him what you must to go with you to the place Peter was killed. Raise Peter and find out what he knew."

"What he knew about what, Tallman? Do not be angry. Tell me what is needed so that I may not fail you again. Please, Tallman, tell your good servant what to do. . . ."

The polelike form turned impatiently. "What did the youth know of 'magicians'? What did he know about 'Council'? What was he plotting with the wizards? Find out, Laggy Nap. Return here as soon as may be or burn, Laggy Nap. I will not be patient."

I watched him retreat through the sagging gates, slumping, watched him take the small wain which the Dupies had already hitched for him and mount to the seat, there to hold the reins lax-ly in his hands as though he had never seen them before. He turned to call rebelliously, "Tallman. Give me Izia, at least. She is good with the beasts and will make sure I reach Betand in time. . . ."

"Go, Laggy Nap. I have another use in mind for Izia."

The little wagon rolled out through the gates and away down the long line of hills toward the north. Still Dolwys' foot was upon my own, his jaw next to mine chewing endlessly at nothing. It was hard, hard with Izia lying there not five paces from me, weeping upon her hands, the Dupies capering about her as they made sorcerous motions with their plump little hands.

"Oh, pretty, pretty, all for Dupies, this one. Oh, we will love it to death, pretty legs, pretty legs . . ."

I shuddered, somehow aware of what it was the Tallman planned, so hideous a thing, and yet it came into my mind as though Didir had plucked it from the Tallman's head. I would stop it, stop it, but the need was not yet, for Tallman called the Dupies away to unload the wagons which Nap had left behind. They called into play a kind of metal creature with arms and a clattering track for feet which helped them, and Fatman carried some things to and fro. There was ore of a kind so special that they picked up even tiny fragments of it dropped from the sacks; bottles and jars of stuff I did not recognize; long bundles of herbs with an odor which reminded me of Windlow's herb garden in that land far to the south. Soon they had unloaded all the wagons except the little cold-cart which Nap had told me contained perishable fruits. All the sacks and bundles were heaped on that strange flat car which Tallman had arrived upon.

Now came a strange hiatus.

Tallman went to the cold-cart, walked around it, lifted its covering, touched it here and there. Behind him the monsters wheeled and capered, silent as shadows. The hood hid whatever passed for Tallman's face, but the angle of his head spoke of concentration. At last he spoke.

"You are a good hitch, you Fatman, you Dupies. I chose well to choose you from the monster pits as my hitch. You did well to warn me that the Trader had not brought everything, Fatman. I had time to find out what to do . . . what questions to ask."

The tenor Dupey said, "Tallman? Will *they* be angry? *They* will be angry, won't they?"

The lofty head nodded, once, twice.

"But Dupey still gets the legs, don't we, Tallman? Dupey gets the pretty legs to have. Oh, we'll put them in the coldwagon, Tallman. They'll last a long time in the coldwagon."

The lofty head turned toward Izia, spoke softly. "I said you would be rewarded, Dupey. So you shall." Then, voice raised, "Do you know your fate, woman? Dupey does not care whether you know or not, but I enjoy it more when the fate is known and the one shaped like *them* can suffer in knowing what will happen." The pole-like form shifted from side to side, as though blown by an unfelt wind. "Dupey has two heads, as you have observed. Two sets of arms, two upper bodies. However, he has only one set of hips and legs. He needs another set, obviously. He prefers a female set, for reasons of his own, eh, Dupey?" The monster capered, patted his cheeks, kissed himself, busied himself about his lower body with both sets of hands. Peter, water ox, could not watch. Dolwys's foot pressed upon me.

"Give me," cried Dupey in two voices. "Give me."

"He has various ways of removing the top half," mused the Tallman. "Dupey is original, innovative. I have been much amused by watching Dupey."

"Dupey was saved," the monster cried. "Saved from the horrid midwifes. Saved to serve Tallman and *them*. Weren't we, Tallman? Oh, give me . . ."

"Patience, patience, Dupies. First you must unload the cold-wagon. Otherwise you will have nowhere to keep the pretty legs. . . ." Some other sound came from Tallman, some sound of humor. Compared to that sound, laughter is the song of angels. Such a sound devils might make.

But with that sound the cover was thrown back from the chill wagon, and long bundles were brought from it and laid in a single, close layer upon the car. Something about the size and shape of those bundles picked at a mind horrified by Tallman, petrified by monsters, picked at a mind without result. But then Dupey turned too quickly from his work, and the covering of one of the bundles caught upon his belt. He turned to cover the contents of the bundle again, quickly, but the water ox which was Peter had seen, seen, seen. It was Windlow, old Windlow lying there, ash gray with cold, unmoving. It all happened too fast, too fast for Peter or Dolwys to react, for Tallman was once more on the car, the pawns were summoned to sit upon its edges, and it was moving away through the tower mouth which had rumbled open. Fatman was watching Dupey. Dupey was approaching Izia. Peter fought to be in two places at once, but it was too late. The tower door mumbled shut.

Water oxen have horns, usually blunted. They have huge, slow feet. They are ponderous, quiet, seldom moved to anger. Therefore, what Dolwys and I became might not have been called water oxen but something else, not totally unlike. Our horns were needle sharp, our feet hard and hooved, our anger real. Dupey never reached the place where Izia lay. Fatman was spilled from his wagon long before he reached the tower door he wheeled for. Beneath the trampling hooves they became mere broken clots of shadow upon the hard pavement within the darkness of the spidery arches. When we had done my heart was pounding as though we had fought a great battle, and it was almost with surprise that I turned to see Izia still upon the ground, mouth open in bleak astonishment.

It was furred-Peter and long-legged Dolwys who brought her up the steep slopes to the pinnacle where Mavin waited. Perhaps she had been watching us from her bird form, for it needed little explanation to tell her what had happened. Izia fell away from our supporting arms to curl upon the stone, turned into herself as a snail turns, tight against the world. The seared, horrid skin of her legs lay bare, an obscene statement of her life with Laggy Nap. Dolwys and I sat panting until I could speak.

"Windlow's body, Mavin. Brought by Nap, in the wagon. The Tallman took it. Through those doors. We didn't have time to . . . I'll have to go back."

"But we need a Healer for her," said Dolwys. "We must do something for the girl!"

"We have a Healer," said Mavin, fixing me with her raptor's eyes. "That is, we have one if Peter chooses to use it. . . ."

I was so breathless, so senseless, that it took me a time to realize what she meant. Dealpas. First among Healers. Among the Gamesman of Barish in my pocket.

"Of course," I stuttered. "At once, I'll . . ."

"Shhh," she said. "Take a moment to get your breath. She will not perish in the next moment what she has survived for the past years." She went to the woman and knelt beside her, urging Izia to her feet, into the cave and onto the bed there, pressing a hot brew into her hands, all despite Izia's incomprehension and blank-eyed apathy. The sight of her legs had done what all the years of Laggy Nap had not, driven her into a kind of madness.

"What if Dealpas cannot heal her?" I murmured, to no one in particular. It was Swolwys who answered me as he brought me some of that same brew which Mavin was spooning into Izia.

"Well, and what if the Healer cannot? Or you cannot? Then she must live or die with what is, as we all must. It will not lie upon your shoulders, Peter. If blame be found, let it be found on Nap's hands."

"You could go further back than that," I said bitterly. "To the Shifter who sold Izia when she was only a child. She could not have been more than seven or eight then. Taken from Game knows where; sold for Game knows what reason."

"Do not say 'Shifter' in that tone," Swolwys demanded. "It could have been a Seer, or a Tragamor, or a pawn, for all that. Each plays his Game, and Games eat men. They eat children, also, but it is the Game does it, not the Gamesman."

"Some Gamesmen do," I said, thinking of Mandor, and Nap, and the fat Duke of Betand. Swolwys was right, though. I did tend to think ill of Shifters, both because of Schlaizy Noithn and because of . . . Yarrel. What brought Yarrel to mind? I had not seen him since he walked away from me outside Bannerwell, giving up our friendship, turning his back on me. His face swam into my mind, dark hair, level brows, large-nosed and generous-lipped. I pressed my hands to my face and shook myself. Now was not the time to indulge in this bittersweet nostalgia. I went into the cave.

"Let me try Dealpas," I said to Mavin. "Though it may not work. Silkhands the Healer told me that tissue, once dead, cannot be healed."

Mavin had uncovered Izia's legs and was studying them as I spoke. The boots had come high upon her thighs, almost to the crotch, and there was a line around her thighs there, healthy pink glow of flesh above, gray scabrous hide below, like a diseased lizard. "I do not think the tissue is dead," she said. "I think the boots did not really burn at all, but acted directly upon the nerves. This flesh is abnormal, but it lives. . . ."

"Well, let us hope Dealpas will know." I reached into the

pocket to find the little Gamesman. I had to search among them.
Dealpas did not come into my hand readily. My fingers chased
her among the other pieces, catching her finally against my
flesh. She came reluctantly, slowly, with infinite regret.

"I thought I had left all this," I felt her say. "Pain. Suffer-
ing. I thought I was done with it. . . ."

"There is never an end," said Didir.

"Never," echoed Dorn.

And from the others within I heard agreement, according to
their natures. There was Wafnor's sturdy cheer, Shattnir's cold
challenge, Trandilar's passion. And among them Dealpas stood
as one weeping.

I was firm. "Come, there is work here."

"There is always work." But she came, regretfully, until I
laid my hands on Izia's flesh, and then she was as a rushing
stream.

I could not follow what it was she did. It was like Shifting in a
way, for filaments seemed to flow from my own hands into the
flesh of Izia. It was like Moving, in a way, for once there the filaments stretched and tasted and smelled at things, chased down
long white bundles of fiber, paddled through blood, marched
unerringly along great columns of bone. It was easy to find the
wrongness, less easy to set it right. Expeditions went out into
far-flung territories of gut and fluid, into intimate halls of gland,
bubbling hotly in wrinkled caverns, to return with this and that
thing, to pump and build and stretch, to open cell walls and herd
things, as a herdsman his flock, which twinkled and spun like
stars, to clamp upon sparkling nerves so that no hint of pain
could move past the place it originated. I watched, sniffed,
tasted, and was one with Dealpas. I learned. I would have to
have been witless not to have learned, but withal that learning I
could tell there was a universe she knew and I never would.

Until, after a long time, she separated herself from me and
became what she had been, a withdrawing presence, a mind
which demanded to be let alone, to rest, to sleep, never to be
wakened.

The others let her go. I let her go. Before me on the pallet,
Izia's flesh appeared not greatly different from what it had been
before, but my hands told me healing was begun. Enough. She
slept. I knew she would sleep long. Her face had relaxed into

quiet, and she lay with mouth a little open, faintly snoring, a little bubble at the corner of her mouth. I knew with unshakable certainty where I had seen that face before and why it was I had been so drawn to her.

"She is so like Yarrel," I whispered. "So like that she can be no one other than his sister, his lost sister, the one he thought dead, gone in the Game, lost to a Shifter. He hated me for that. But she is not dead. No."

"Are you certain?" Mavin asked. Her words were nonsense. I had just said I was certain.

I stroked the hot forehead, pushed the dark hair back from her face. Yarrel had worn his so, brushed back from his face.

"She must go back to him," I said. "To her family. As soon as possible."

"So long ago. Will she remember her family at all?"

"No matter. What she cannot remember, she will relearn. But she must go back, at once."

"You can take her," said Mavin. "When she wakes."

"No. Swolwys may take her, or Dolwys, or both. In fact, they must, for she must be kept utterly safe, beyond all possibility of harm. I cannot take her myself. I must go after Windlow."

For if anything was certain, it was sure that I could not fail Windlow and Himaggery again. I had failed them once in the Bright Demesne, once in the Blot. But not again.

8

The Magicians

I was surprised when Mavin said she would go with me. I had always thought of her, when I thought of her, as elsewhere, not with me. When I had met her on the pinnacle, it had been with no thought that she would accompany me anywhere. If I had had any expectations of that meeting, it would have been to spend some time with her, in her own place, and learn what I could from her to make my Shifterish soul more comfortable. So, when she said very calmly that the twins would escort Izia to her childhood home and she would come with me, I was speechless for a time. Remnants of courtly training suggested I should protect her by refusing her company. Good sense told me how silly that was. Of the two of us, she was probably better able to take care of herself. Certainly she had had far more experience than I. At the end, I said nothing, not even thanks.

"I would have gone eventually anyhow," she said, over Izia's sleeping form. "The time has come to find out what happens beyond the Blot. Many of us have known for a long time that strangeness and disturbance comes from there. If you saw Windlow's body, then it is certain Himaggery is there as well. Do you think they are alive?" She did not wait for my nod, we had been over this before. "Himaggery, yes, and probably Throsset of Dowes, that great Sorcerer, and Mind-Healer Talley, one of the few Healers ever to have great skill in healing sick minds, and who knows—a thousand more who have disappeared. Pawns as well, I suppose. I have seen them go by the dozens into that place like dazed sheep. Into the mumble mouths, riding the little cars. Many of us know, have known, but we have not been organized. . . . No. We have simply been too fearful to go into that place.''

"You? Fearful?'' I doubted this.

"Do not mistake my arrogance for courage, my son. It is true that I am renowned for what I can do. But I am afraid of the unknown, as are most men, Gamesmen or pawns alike. My sisters and I were told as children that monsters dwelt in the West, that night creatures would come from there to take us if we were naughty, that all darkdreams came from the West. When I grew older, I learned that there was truth in that. Of course I fear it. We should both fear it, but there is at least one place worse than this!''

"And we will go?''

"Of course.''

Swolwys and Dolwys were not so sure. They gave her arguments which extended into the night, all the while that Izia slept. I went now and then to see that she was covered and to look at her legs. The grayness was fading. There were patches of smooth skin behind her knees and along the ankles. I gave thanks to Dealpas in my heart, but did not summon her. I remembered the skipping chant which the children of Schooltown used to sing beneath the windows of Mertyn's House, as they sang in every village of the world. "Pain's maid, broken leaf, Dealpas, heart's grief.'' There was a verse for each of the eleven, so familiar to all children that we did not even think of it as anything religious or special. I thought of others. "Mind's mistress, moon's wheel, cobweb Didir, shadow-steel.'' That one was right enough, a web of adamant woven from moonlight and shadow. "Only-free and sent-far, trickiest is Thandbar.'' I hoped that one was right, too, for we two of Thandbar's kindred. From what Mavin had said about the Blot, we would need to be tricky. I was frightened, too, but I did not hesitate except to stroke Izia's hair and touch her cheek. I knew then that I loved her, but I was not sure whether I loved her because she was Yarrel's sister or because she was herself. It did not matter. I might never see her again after the morrow.

When she woke, I sat at her side and held her hands in mine, though she cowered and tried to jerk them away. I made her look at her legs, at the places which were healing, made her listen as I told her that she was healing, healing, that all of the years with Laggy Nap were past, gone, done with, forever dissolved in time. She shivered and sobbed, at last letting her hands lie in mine. Only then I asked, "Do you remember a time before Laggy Nap? Do you remember when you were a child?"

"I remember horses," she said.

I laughed to myself. Oh, assuredly this was Yarrel's sister.

"Do you remember a boy, your own age? A brother?" I wanted her to name him. Oh, I held my breath wanting her to name him.

"I remember Dorbie," she said. "Dorbie was my fusty."

"No, Izia. Not a fustigar. A boy. A brother. What was his name?"

Her eyes became unfocused, concentrating. "It was . . . was Yarry," she said at last. "Yarry was my brother. Twin. Twins we were." Years welled to spill down her cheeks. "I lost him. I lost everything."

"No." I squeezed her hands, kept myself from hugging her, for I knew it would only frighten her and remind her of Laggy Nap. "No, Izia. They aren't lost. Tomorrow you will travel with my cousins to find Yarry, and your parents." Later I cursed myself for mentioning her parents. I had not heard of Yarrel's family in a year. One or both might be dead. Well, it was too late to change the words. "Your family are still there, Izia, and they have never ceased thinking of you."

"Oh, fool, fool," she said, singsong. "They sold me to the Shifter. They did not care for me." The sobbing commenced again.

"Shhh. Izia, that was Laggy Nap's lies, all lies. You were not sold to the Shifter. He took you, by guile, by trickery. Try to remember how he took you! It was the Shifter who did it, Izia, no one else."

She subsided onto the pallet, and I gave way to Mavin who brought yet another cup of hot broth from the fire, her cure for all ills, to be spooned down the girl's throat a few drops at a time. She shook her head, made a bitter face as though she tasted gall when she saw Izia crying. Later she said much to me about Gamesmen who prey upon children. She needed have said none of it. I already had my opinions, and she could not have made them worse.

By noon Izia was enough recovered to finger the healing places on her legs with trembling hands, to seem to understand when we told her she was to return to Yarrel, even to be eager to depart. Mavin took some time, more than I thought necessary, to tell her that Dolwys and Swolwys were "good Shifters" who would see that she was kept safe. She also spent some time with my cousins, instructing them how they should behave toward her to avoid hurting her further. Swolwys went into the plains to fetch horses. When he returned, Izia became herself once more, walking about the animals, picking up a foot to examine a hoof, all the actions I had seen her perform in Nap's camp. So, they went away, and Mavin and I were left alone.

"I had thought," she began with a brooding stare into the darkness of the Blot, "that we would take the shape of those two creatures you dispatched down there. I can manage the duplicate creature if you can manage the shape of the Fatman."

I considered it. When we had destroyed Fatman, we had not much damaged the Fatwagon, and I thought I could figure out how to run it. I could not imagine taking the shape of the Dupies, however, and I asked Mavin how she would manage that.

"I will keep myself low, in the belly, I should think, with bony plates around my brain. The heads of the creature will have to be managed like puppets. With practice, I should be able to make both of them speak at once, though that may not be necessary." Still she brooded, finally swearing a horrible oath and stepping from her perch. "I don't like it. It is like taking a shape of shame. The Guild of Midwives has much to answer for."

"Not their fault," I said. "The Dupies said they had been 'saved from the horrible Midwives.' I did not understand what they meant at the time. . . ."

She shook her head. "It has to do with the oaths the Midwives take, Peter. With their religion, if you will. I find myself more in sympathy with it, the older I grow." She saw my puzzled look and went on. "Do you think you have a—a soul?"

Windlow, Silkhands, Yarrel and I had discussed this at Windlow's tower in the southlands, in a recent time which seemed very long ago. It was old Windlow who had pointed out that each of us was conscious of being two persons, one which did and one which observed the doing. He had told us it was this which made mankind different from the animals we knew. So, I considered Mavin's question and said, "I have more, perhaps, than a fustigar. Or so Windlow thought."

"The Midwives believe in the soul. However, they do not believe that it is inborn in mankind. They believe it comes partly with the learning of language (which mankind alone of the animals seems to have) and partly from our fellowmen, a gift of human society to each child. Do you think that sensible?"

"I'm not sure I follow," I said. "You mean, if I had been born among fustigars, and reared by fustigars, learning no language, I would be more fustigar than human?"

"Something like that. But more. The Midwives believe that only those who perceive their own humanity and perceive that *others* have the same become ensouled. Some who look like men can never believe that others are like themselves. They do not believe that others are real. One such was Mandor. . . ."

I nodded. I believed her. Mandor had seen the whole world as his fingernail, to be cut at will and the parings thrown away.

"Huld, too," she went on. "Though he talks a mockery of manners. The soulless ones can be well-mannered, as a beast may be well-mannered. Or so say the midwives who have studied the matter."

"What has this to do with Dupey?"

"Ah." She came to herself with a start. "The Midwives take an oath, very solemn and binding, that they will look into the future of each child born, and if they do not see that one gaining a soul, then they do not let it live. It is the Talent of the Midwives to see the future in that way, more narrowly than do Seers, and more reliably. It is called the Mercy-gift, the gift the Midwife gives the child, to look into the future and find there that it will have gained a soul."

"How explain Mandor, then, or Huld?"

"The great Houses want no Midwife at their childbeds. No. They care nothing for 'souls.' They care only for manners, and this they can train into any if they be but strict enough. However, I do not think the Dupey was the offshoot of any great House. More likely he was scavenged from the Midwives, or born in some House where Midwives did not go." This last was said with a hesitating fall, as thought she knew where that might have been. The talk was depressing me, but it had raised a question I had to ask.

"And did the Midwives deliver me, Mother?"

She smiled such a smile, a dawning on her face. "Oh, they did, Peter. And you have had all the gifts we could give you, Mertyn and I. No fear. You are no Mandor. Nor any Dupey. If men all were better, perhaps even a Dupey could be given a soul, but it would take holymen and women to do it. No simple mother could do it. The horror would be too great, and the pain of the child too monstrous to bear. How did he live? And why? While it is true that monstrous things are sometimes born, it takes something more monstrous, evil, and prideful yet to keep them alive. . . ."

"And the Fatman?" I asked. "Legless, he was, with no lower body at all. Had he been born that way, he would have died unless someone intervened. Why? How and why? Well, perhaps Windlow can tell us, for he is very wise. . . ."

"If we can find him. If we can free him. If he yet lives. Well, we will not do it standing here. It is time to go."

We stayed only long enough to set a boulder before Mavin's cave. There were things inside which she treasured. We went empty-handed, clad only in our fur until we reached the puddled shadows of the Blot. There clouds of flies rose from the remnants of Dupey and Fatman. There we took those shapes and moved about in them, trying them. They were hateful. They were *wrong*. There was no logic or kindness in those shapes, and I began to understand what Mavin had tried to say about souls. One could not exist in those shapes without becoming compressed, warped, envenomed. There was pain intrinsic to the shape, and I began to think what it would be like to live with that pain forever. I began to modify the shape to shut the pain away, and I heard Mavin panting.

"I cannot inhabit it," she said. "I must carry it upon me like a rigging. . . ."

"Perhaps we should try something else," I offered.

"No," she said. "My mistake was in trying to take the identity of the creature. We must only *appear* to be these creatures. We must not *be* these things or we will become monstrously changed."

So, we were warned, and I was glad for the time spent in

moving and trying that body. It took time, but at last we were able to make an appearance not unlike what had been before while still maintaining our own identities untouched. I was as weary as though I had run twelve leagues.

"Rest," said Mavin. "Here is food. We will carry some with us, for Gamelords know what will be found within."

Even in those few moments rest, we found that we shifted away from those shapes. Mavin barked a short laugh.

"Mavin Manyshaped," she mocked herself. "I do not deserve the name."

I thought of the shapes I had taken easily, almost without trying. "It is not lack of Talent," I told her, sure that I was right, feeling it through some internal shrinking as though my spirit shrank from what I was. "The shapes are evil, Mavin. Moreover, they were meant to be evil."

She did not contradict me, and we went toward the mumble mouth in those evil shapes, building within ourselves certain barriers against becoming what we appeared to be. I do not know how Mavin managed. For myself, I built a kind of shell between me and the image of Fatman, and within that shell dwelt Peter and the Gamesmen of Barish, within and yet no part of that thing.

Mavin had evidently observed the Blot for some time, for she knew how to open the mouths by striking them sharply with a stick, crying in the Dupey's voice, "Open, open, old silly thing. Open and let Dupies come in. . . ."

There were shriekings and clatterings from within, and then the mouth opened to extrude its long metal tongue. Grooved tracks divided it lengthwise, tracks into which the flatcar had fit. The Fatwagon did not fit these, but I managed to straddle them with my own wheels as I followed the Dupey shape up the ramp and into the place beyond. I had expected a tunnel, a place not unlike the catacombs beneath Bannerwell. This place was not what I had expected.

The walls were metal, long sheets of it, dim and slightly glossy, polished at one time but now faintly fogged with time. At intervals the metal was interrupted by panels of glass, many of them broken, the shards lying upon the floor of the way. Behind some of the intact glasses were greenish lights, feeble, sickly lights. It was enough to find one's way by, not truly enough to see by, so we strained to see, pushed at the dimness with our minds, grew fractious and annoyed in the effort. Above us the metal panels extended to a high, curved ceiling, and in this were screened holes emitting sighs and drips, moody winds and dampness smelling of rot. Something in the place tried to help us by lighting the way ahead, darkening the way behind. Each effort was accompanied by frustrated clicks and whirrings, often with no result except to plunge us into darkness. Then there would be running noises, hummings, squeals as of slaughtered belts or gears, and light would come again, only to go off again when it was most inconvenient.

"Gamelords," said Mavin in fury. "Why can't the place ignore us and let us be." At the sound of her voice the clickings and hummings redoubled in inefficient clatter. She stopped, forehead furrowed. "It hears me."

"Tell it to turn the lights on and leave them on," I grated between my teeth. At my words the spotty lights went on down the whole length of the corridor and all the noises stopped. We looked at one another, expecting some other thing to happen, but silence succeeded silence, dripping water fell behind us, small breezes beat damply into our faces. We went on. The lights stayed on and there were no more of the noises. "Someone heard us," I said.

"Something heard us," she corrected. "This is a place of magicians. A place of mechanisms. Like the machine which unloaded the cargo, things created to fulfill special functions. . . ."

"They do not do it well," I commented, half angrily. The wheels of the Fatwagon had begun to squeal. Mavin reached over with the can of oil she had taken from Dupey's body and the squeak faded to a high shriek at the very limits of perception. It set my teeth on edge. Our journey was not helped by the fact that we had come to side corridors, branching ways, each helpfully lit into dim distances.

"The tracks," Mavin said, noting my confusion. I saw then that the grooves in the floor did not go into the side corridors. I flushed. I should have seen that, as she had. We went on, as quietly as we could, the endless corridor fading behind us into phosphorescent distance, an equal tunnel always ahead, no change, no variation except in the pattern of broken glass or the shape of the puddles under the dripping vents. We had brought food with us. Twice we stopped to fetch it forth and nibble as we went on. My internal clock said that half a day had gone, or more. The corridor did not seem to curve, and we had walked far enough to come under the mountains which had been visible from the pinnacle.

"Snowfast Range," Mavin said. "We call them the Forbidden Mountains, full of glaciers and crevasses. We have a long history of explorers going into the Snowfasts and not returning. . . ."

Then we stopped, confused. The tracks divided into three before us, one going on down the endless corridor, another swerving right down a long declivity, one going left up a long slope into the dark. I could not kneel, so Mavin did, peering at the tracks to see which ones evidenced wear, which were dimmed with corrosion. She gestured us off to the left. When we entered that way, the lights came on, fewer of them than in the way we had left, but still enough that we could avoid stumbling over the fragments of ceiling which littered the middle of the way.

Now side corridors led off with increasing frequency. We began to hear sounds, murmurs, buzzing as of machinery or distant voices in conversation. Mavin began a little song, silly and repetitive, the kind of thing the Dupies would have sung for themselves, discordantly twin-voiced. She had mastered the shape at last and was able to make both heads move and speak. From deep within me the voice of Didir came in a faint sigh, "Persons, nearing, beware. . . ." I passed the warning on to Mavin, who needed it not. Neither of us were surprised when we were confronted, though both of us took pains to simulate paroxysms of hysteria as we knew our shapes would have done.

Black they were, pale faces showing like moons against the dark, bodies and limbs hidden beneath the straight black dresses they wore, hair and ears hidden beneath square black caps which rode upon their heads like balanced boxes, held there by tight cloths which came down over the ears, under the throat, down the back of the neck. Around each wrist was a metal band, and upon each hand a fingerless glove. Against all that black the fingers squirmed like worms in gravesoil, and the faces peered at us without expression. We backed away, gibbering in our pretended fright, and one of them spoke.

"Well, Shear, monsters escaped from the pits? How come here? And why?"

"I have no idea, Dean Manacle. None. But they are not going from the pits, you will note, but toward them. . . ."

Mavin chose this moment to say, "Oh, Dupies need to talk to Tallman, good Tallman will help Dupies. Dupies got into the mumble mouths, we did, came to find Tallman. . . ."

"Oh, do not be in a temper, great sirs," I managed to gulp. "The calling machine did not function, and we have word. . . ."

"Dupies say 'Patience, patience'," Mavin went on, wickedly. "Fatman says we must find Tallman, oh, good Tallman, to tell Dupies what to do. . . ."

"Creatures from some portal," said the one called Shear. "That is why they go toward the pits. Creatures from some portal who have come into the base in search of their hitch."

"An inescapable hypothesis, Shear. Also, an interesting occurrence. One worthy of note. Perhaps a small monograph? However, practicality dictates that they not be allowed to remain *here*. Will you call for removers?"

"Certainly, Dean Manacle. As you wish."

It was as though they heard nothing we said, as though we had chirped like birds or howled like fustigars to make some general noise without content. Mavin realized it as soon as I did, and we both subsided into meaningless babble. They took no notice of this, either. The one called Shear fiddled with a wrist band, poking at tiny knobs upon it with a fierce display of concentration which even I could recognize as mannered. Who were these strange ones? Mavin made a face at me from Dupey's left head and went on with the nonsense sound she was making. The two before us continued to converse as though we were not there.

We had not long to play this game. A shrill shrieking set Fatman's ears on edge. I damped the sound, a sound which seemed to accompany every machine which moved in this place. A little cart came gravely around a corner, ridden by two replicas of Tallman, or perhaps by one replica and Tallman himself. It did not matter, for the one called Manacle made it clear there was no difference, no distinction.

"Tallmen! There are two monsters here, probably from a portal. See they are removed and that the Tallman responsible is sent to the pits. . . ."

The Tallmen did not reply. I began to understand that the black-dressed ones, who must be those magicians we had heard so much of, did not hear words unless spoken by one of their own kind. The treelike figures merely unfolded themselves from the cart and reached toward us with their hands. A bolt of force, small and controlled, but nonetheless painful, struck us both. We cried out, both Dupey heads in unison and Fatman in shock and surprise, a long harmonic of anguish. We moved in the direction indicated.

"Tallman," I cried, "Fatman has news, news, listen Tallman to what Fatman has to say. . . ."

One of them spoke, not quite the voice I had heard before. "Hold your noise, monsters. We are not your hitch. He will be found, you may be sure, and disciplined beside you in the pits. Were you not told never to enter the labyrinth! You were told. All the hitches are told. Now you have made *them* angry." Another, totally gratuitous, bolt struck us from behind though we were moving as rapidly as possible. I conceived a hatred for the Tallmen in that moment. Vengeance would have to come later, however, for now it was enough that we were being escorted into the maze. I comforted myself with this while Shifting my burned flesh about. The bolts had been painful enough, but they had not done any real damage.

The Tallmen did not speak between themselves. All was quiet except for the shrieking wheels of the cart, the drip of water from the ceiling, the moody sighing of the ducts. Soon the ceilings began to rise; we came to larger spaces; we encountered other carts and other black-clad magicians striding along the corridors without seeming to notice what went on around them. Then, almost without warning, we were at the pits. They opened before us, broad and deep as quarries, sheer walls dropping into a swarm of ceaseless movement as of a hive of insects overturned. A cage of metal stood at the pit wall, tall metal beams which reached from the pit floor to the ceiling far above, and within this square of beams a smaller cage was suspended. We were forced inside; the door was shut behind us; the endless machine shriek began as were lowered into the swarm where a

thousand creatures like ourselves flurried in ceaseless agitation.
The door opened to let us out, and we moved hesitantly into
nightmare. Beside me I heard Mavin's voice from Dupey's
throat. "Gamelords! What madness is this?"

They crawled about us, oozed, flopped, hopped or stumbled,
by every means of locomotion and by none. Some had one leg
and some had none, or three, or six. Some were one-headed,
some had two, or none, or four. There were blobs which lay
while features chased themselves across their surfaces; some attached to mechanisms which made the Fatwagon seem a model
of simplicity. There were howlers, moaners, silent ones whose
thoughts beat at me in a tide of agony. The place stank of refuse,
and excrement, and blood. Some things, dead and half eaten,
lay against the walls of the place. Instinctively Mavin and I
moved to the wall and put our backs against it. I looked up to see
the hooded heads of the Tallmen peering down at us. I had never
seen a Tallman's face, and I wondered in that instant if they had
faces. Some of the creatures around us did not. Something
crawled across my feet and lay there, rippling at me. Deep within, I heard Didir recoil. "Wrongness, Peter. Wrongness. Beware, beware."

The walls of the pit were pierced with black arches, screens
behind which we could discern faint shadows, black on black.
A bell rang somewhere, and the creatures began to edge toward
these arches. There were troughs beneath them which began to
flow with half liquid soup. The creatures fed. I watched, feeling
the place with my skin. It was like being in a waking dream, a
dream from which one knows one should be able to waken. The
cage rattled upward, then down once more. Inside it was a
Tallman and great bundles of solid food, stinking sides of meat,
sacks of beaten grain. The Tallman came from the cage before it
tipped to spill the food upon the floor. When the cage rattled upward again, the monsters broke from the arches, howling, to de-
scend upon the scattered food. The Tallman kept away from
them, turning, turning until glittering eyes from beneath the
concealing hood met mine.

"Fatman," he breathed. "I will kill you. . . ." He moved
toward me. I let him come close, close enough that he could not
be seen from above. Then Wafnor reached out and held him,

bound him about with arms of steel, held him fast while I looked under that hood at his eyes. Tallmen had faces, of a sort. At least, this one did. The face burned hatred at me and at Dupey behind me. "Who are you?" it asked at last. "You are not Fatman."

"No," I admitted. "I am not Fatman. I am one who will hear you talk, Tallman. Tell me of this place, of these magicians, of these pits. . . ."

He was not willing to do so, but it did not matter. Didir Read him; Wafnor shook words out of him; Trandilar entranced him. The bell rang again. The creatures assembled before the arches once again, and I looked with a Shifter's eyes through that dark glass to the shadows beyond. Pale, moon faces were there under their square hats; younglings were there, dressed in black but with soft caps covering their heads, eyes wide and fingers busy as they wrote on little pads of paper, wrote and peered, wrote and peered.

"What are they doing?" I demanded.

"Monster watching," Tallman gasped. "It is what they do. It is why they say they are here."

I thought this a lie, and yet Didir said Tallman believed it to be true. Since they were watching us, we behaved as monsters should, howled, bubbled, rocked and capered, all the while holding Tallman fast so that he could not move. Those watching would have only seen him stand, head down, face obscured. After a time the bell rang once more, the monsters left the arches to resume their endless movement in the pit.

We questioned. At last, we knew all the Tallman knew and let him go. He backed away from us to the center of the pit, staring about him with wild, glittering eyes, maddened by shadows. They were not shadows who came after him, however, but things of the pit which seemed to bear Tallmen some malice. He had a weapon of some kind, and he did some damage to them before he was buried beneath their bodies. Mavin and I did not watch. We were intent upon those other Tallmen who hovered at the edge of the pit, far above.

"He did not harm his hitch," said one. "I would have killed mine had they disobeyed me. Why did he not kill his hitch?"

"Mad," said the other. "He was mad. Sometimes we go

mad, you know. They say so.''

"I would have killed them,'' replied the first. ''Mad or not.''
They moved away from the pit and were gone. I caught a Dupey
eye upon me with Mavin's keen intelligence behind it.

"We have spent time enough here,'' she hissed.

There was the matter of the Fatwagon, which should be left in
a place it would not attract attention. There was the matter of the
arches behind which the watchers lurked. She knew this as well
as I, and we sought a solution to the dilemma. We found it at the
base of the metal cage, a slight declivity in the pit wall, a space
large enough to hide us as we Shifted. When next the moveable
cage fell and rose, we rose with it, hidden beneath it like a false
bottom to the thing. Once the space around the pit was empty,
two Tallmen came into being and moved away to the fringing
corridors.

When we had found a secluded place, we stopped to set some
plan of action. Tallman had believed what he had told us. He
had not known the name ''Himaggery'' or ''Windlow.'' He
knew only that a certain cargo was ordered for *them*, that it
would go behind the inner doors to *them*, to be used in certain
ceremonies which were to happen soon. He knew only that the
monsters were created by *them*, in order that the monsters could
be watched by *them*.

They made things, things which were sent out into the world
to be sold or given away by the Gifters. *They* needed pawns to
serve them, so pawns were brought in through the mumble
mouths. Tallmen were created by *them* to maintain the corridors, to maintain the portals, to repair things which broke. ''But
we cannot,'' he had said pitiably. ''No one knows how to fix
them. . . .''

They did not talk to Tallmen, except to give instructions.
This Tallman had not been through the inner doors; he did not
know what happened there. We asked what friends he had?
None. What acquaintances? None. Surely he slept somewhere,
in some company? No. At most, they could gather in pairs.
Why sleep in company? Why eat in company? One slept wherever one was. . . .

We had asked him how he had learned to speak? Surely he remembered a childhood?

At that his eyes had rolled back in his head and he had trembled like a drumhead. Mavin had said sadly, "Let it go, Peter. I do not know whether it was born of human kind, but it has been changed beyond recognition. This is only an empty vessel, drained of all but limited speech and directed action and fear of pain. Let it go."

That was when we had let him go.

Now we leaned against a wall and considered. Somewhere in this tangled, underground labyrinth were the inner doors the Tallman had spoken of. Somewhere in this web of a place we would find some answers, but we would not find them standing against a wall. We would have to follow some of *them*. "I will not do this," Mavin said with asperity, "mock that unfortunate creature by saying *them*. They are magicians, and so I will say."

"Say away," I commented. "Particularly if it will help some."

Easier conceived of than accomplished. There were none of the magicians about. Perhaps it was not a time they moved about. Perhaps the earlier occurrence had been a random happening with little chance of repetition. We wandered, baffled and frustrated. Bells rang. Machines wheezed and gulped. Tallmen moved quietly past. Silence came.

"Perhaps it is night outside," said Mavin. "These beings must once have lived beneath the sun. Perhaps they keep its time still."

"If that is so, they may be sleeping rather than watching what goes on around them. And if that is so, then we might risk other bodies than these." We hesitated, wondering whether it was wise to take the risk.

At last she said, "If it finds us anything, it is worth it. I will go left, you right, as fast and as far as possible. Meet here when they begin to move about again."

So we agreed, and I set out as furred-Peter once more, on legs as swift as I could Shift them. I had no luck, none, and returned to the place heavy with anger and disappointment. Mavin was there already, curled against the wall half asleep, and I knew at once she had been luckier than I.

"I found them," she said. "Found the inner doors. Sleep

now, and when we have rested, we will find a way through them.''

We were well hidden. I gave up anger in favor of sleep and dreamed long, too well, of Izia.

9

The Inner Doors

The place of the magicians was full of niches and corners, almost as though they provided space for invisible beings, Tallmen and servants whom they did not see. We found such a niche, a place from which we could see the doors Mavin had found without being seen ourselves. The doors were quite ordinary, a wide pair of time-blotched panels without handles or knobs, and beside them a little booth of glass, though I suspected it was of a material more durable than that. We had not long to wait before one of the magicians came into the booth, an old one, jowls jiggling and pouches beneath his eyes, a nose which, had I seen it in a tavern in Betand, I would have considered evidence of much wine toping. He hawked and mumbled to himself for a time, his voice carried out to us through some contrivance or other which made it echo and boom.

"Huskpaw here," he mumbled. "On duty, Huskpaw. Huskpaw is *on* duty. Doors unlocked. Oh, tum to tum, boredom, weariness, and ennui, clutches and concatenations of all tedium. . . ." Then he must have heard a sound because he stiffened, sat himself down before the glass and took a pose of watchfulness.

We heard the voice of Manacle. "Doctor Manacle, here, Proctor Huskpaw. Desirous of egress . . ."

"What business have you among the monsters?" rapped Huskpaw, so rapidly I knew it was rote, even as he reached for whatever thing it was controlled the doors.

He received a giggle in response, the voice of Shear. "Doctor

Manacle goes forth to select monsters for consecration, Proctor Huskpaw. It is time. The ceremonies will not wait. . . .''

"Lecturer Shear," Manacle's voice, cold as a battlefield after Great Game. "I can make my own explanations, if you please! Huskpaw, give your handle a twist there, my good fellow. Your Dean goes forth among monsters to select a few for consecration. Write me down as upon the business of the college.''

"Certainly, Dean Manacle. At once, sir. Written as upon the business of the college. Surely. Proctor Huskpaw at your convenience, sir. . . .'' opening the doors through which Manacle and Shear emerged, Shear still in a high good humor, obviously unsuppressed. Mavin twitched at me, and we followed them, hearing Huspaw's voice behind us as we went, "Oh, certainly, Dean, certainly, Doctor, Dean Manacle, Dean Mumblehead, Dean monster-lover. Blast and confusion upon him and his lick-ass Shear, old stuff-sox. May he rot. . . .''

We followed the two on a circuitous route before they stopped at last beside one of the monster pits, whether the one we had been in or some other, I could not tell. They leaned at ease upon a railing, looked at the farther wall without letting their eyes move downward, and discussed the grotesques which seethed below.

"Nothing here worth consecration, eh, Shear? Not for us, at any rate. Perhaps for Quench? Now, I have the idea that Quench would select some of these for consecration, don't you?'' Titter, giggle, elbow into the ribs of the shorter magician. "But nothing for us. Pity. That's what comes of being discriminating. Bother and overwork, all to maintain one's standards. . . .'' They wandered off along the corridors, Mavin and I still close behind them in our Tallmen guises. They might have seen us if they had turned, but they did not. They were oblivious to our presence as though they were the only living creatures in all that vast place.

They came to a second pit, or perhaps the same one from another side. Mavin shifted uneasily at my side. The two magicians leaned upon the railing once more and stared at the ceiling fifty manheights above them.

"Now, there are some likely ones here, aren't there, Shear? That three-legged one, yonder, with the tentacles? Most interesting. I must remember to bring that to the attention of my son, Tutor Flogshoulder, to be included in his research. Ah, yes, that one would make interesting watching. One could get a decent footnote out of that. Somehow, however, I do not feel it would be . . . quite . . . right for consecration, do you, Shear?''

Shear, tittering, responding with a shaken head, a flurry of expostulation. ''Not at all, my dear Dean. At least, not for one of your taste and standards. No. Certainly not. For Quench, perhaps. Or for Hurlbar. Not for you. Certainly not . . .''

They were off again. Again we followed. Three times more the scene was repeated. I watched them carefully. They never looked into the pits they talked over. They never saw anything except the featureless walls of the place. It was some kind of Game, perhaps a ritual. I could sense Mavin's impatience, but the play was nearing its close. They had come to a different kind of pit, shallower, cleaner, in a place where the dismal hooting of the ventilators was somewhat muted, the drip from the ceilings somehow stopped. This time the two looked down, and this time they were silent as they looked. Mavin and I faded into an alcove.

''Oh, here are some who will do!'' Manacle, greedy as a child seeing sweets. ''Not well, but better than the others we have examined.''

''Yes.'' Shear in agreement. ''Not perfect, but then, who can expect perfection in these difficult times? Still, better than any of the others we have seen. . . .''

Manacle whistled sharply, and a Tallman materialized at his side out of some corner or cross corridor. There were murmured instructions. The Tallman entered the cage, dropped below my sight. The creak of the rising cage riveted our attention as it squealed its way upward. In it the Tallman stood, surrounded by four little girls.

''No, no, no,'' Manacle cried, full of shrill anger. ''Not that one, idiot. *That* one, over there in the corner. Take this one back and get me *that* one.'' The cage dropped again to return with some exchange made which I could not detect. The little girls were clad in white kilts, not entirely clean, above which their slender chests were as breastless as any baby's. Shear and Manacle gazed at them with greedy satisfaction. ''Oh, these will do very well, won't they, Shear? Bring them along,

Tallman. We will consecrate these monsters at the doors.''
With that they were off, nodding and bubbling in mutual satisfaction and congratulation.

"Monsters?" I whispered to Mavin.

"Females," she said harshly. "Have you seen any female
here, anywhere? The magicians, their servants, the Tallmen, all
are male. These children are the first females I have seen."

"But why 'monsters'? They look perfectly normal to me."

"I think not," she said. "Come, this is our chance to get
through the doors."

She carried out her plan so swiftly I had barely time to make
the shifts with her. First she showed herself to the two children
who were last in line behind the shambling Tallman, cutting
them away from the others and sending them wandering down a
side corridor. Then, we became those children, "conserving
bulk" as she hastily directed, following the Tallman as he
strode along mindlessly, his shadowed face betraying nothing
of interior thought or confusion or misapprehension. I felt
heavy, squeezed into the smaller form, but we managed it well.

At the doors, Huskpaw was instructed to assemble a group of
magicians. There was a good deal of coming and going, lengthy
chanting and waving of papers. The ceremony seemed to be
called "conferring honorary degrees." The two real children
did not respond except to move where they were pushed; Mavin
and I did likewise. The eyes of the real girls showed only a kind
of vacancy, like that of the Tallmen, only more so. I knew then
that they were not normal children but were something else,
perhaps monsters, perhaps something I could not name. Eventually the magicians dropped a robe over each of us, black as
their own, and the ceremony appeared to be over. We were ush-
ered through the doors and into a wide reception chamber where
the group was joined by others to be served with wine and sweet
cakes by a pair of costumed pawns as silent and vacant as the little girls. The girls, we among them, stood in a loose huddle at
one side of the room, largely ignored except for occasional las-
civious glances from Manacle. I was to be grateful for this
seeming invisiblity. I had expected to see only strangers in this
place, and the entrance of someone I knew brought a sudden
terror.

He came through an arched door, dressed much as I had seen

him last at Bannerwell, half helmed as a Demon, clad in silver. Huld: Thalan to Mandor. My tormentor in Bannerwell; him I had conquered and imprisoned in turn. Now, here. In this place. I could not stop an involuntary shudder. He had no reason to suspect I might be here, but I shuddered nonetheless. If he had any cause to suspect, his questing mind would Read me among this multitude and find me in moments. Only the clutter of thoughts in the room hid me now. Within me Didir stirred, whispered, "I will shield you, Peter. Go deep, deep, as you have done before. . . ." I could not take her advice. I had to warn Mavin.

The two little girls were holding hands, clinging together as two kittens might in a strange place. I copied the action, caught Mavin's hand in mine to spell letters into her palm. She stiffened, began to swing her eyes toward him even as I moved before her to screen her from his gaze. Then she saw the Demon helm, and that was enough. Her face went blank, and I knew she was focusing upon some nonsense rhyme, some jibble tune to keep her thoughts busy on the surface, invisible beneath. Didir spoke from within once more, "Go deep, Peter. I will shield you. Watch, listen, but do not be. . . ."

I had done it before, in Bannerwell, had become a witless nothing which wandered about with no more surface thought than a kitchen cat. So I did it now. I became the child whose body I mimicked, became a girl without a mind, a passive body, sank deep into that soft vacancy and listened. Words flowed through my head like water, meaningless as ripples. It did not matter what they meant. When the proper time came, I would remember, or Didir would tell me.

"Huld, my dear fellow." Thus Manacle engaging in rough shoulder pats which caused Huld to tighten his lips and smile angrily. Manacle, not noticing. "Dear fellow. So nice of you to join us. This is an occasion, you know. Signal Day is only two days hence, and it is time to rededicate ourselves to our historic mission. We bring in a few new monsters to serve as breeders, properly consecrated, of course. My position requires me to be first, to set an example. Not the most enjoyable of our duties, but"—manly chuckle—"not the least. Will you join us?"

"May I hope, Dean Manacle, that in the flurry of preparations you have not forgotten why I am here?" Huld, stiff, angry, but with something behind the anger—a kind of gleefulness? Something out of place, something conniving. Didir heard it.

"Certainly not, dear fellow. Of course not. I have transmitted your warnings to several of my colleagues. They are concerned, most concerned. They consider your request quite appropriate, under the circumstances. The Committee will meet tonight, and we will bring the matter before them at that time."

"And you've received the cargo? All of it? That Seer, Windlow, and Himaggery, so-called Wizard? Most important, the young Necromancer, Peter?"

Manacle shifted uncomfortably. "Well now, there's a bit of bother about that. We have two of them, brought in only a few days ago. Yes. But one seems to have been killed en route, so to speak, at least so I am told. The Tallman believed so. He sent the Gifter back to find one of those gamespeople who are supposed to be able to raise the dead. Nothing to that supposition, of course. Impossible to raise the dead. Not like your own talent, my dear Huld, which we have studied and find some signtific basis for. At any rate, the young one isn't in the cargo. . . ."

Huld glared, heat coming off his skin to make Manacle move back from his blazing. "I do not believe he was killed."

"My dear man, the Tallman was quite explicit. The Gifter said a rockfall had completely buried him. No chance of his having survived. Shear, come over here and tell our friend what the Tallman said about that boy who was killed. . . ."

"I don't care what your Tallman said." Huld in fury. "Haven't you understood anything I've said to you? Let me say it again. The Council plots against you, against the magicians. I came to warn you, out of friendship, in return for past favors. The Council works through certain Gamesmen in the outer world. They have done so for decades. Now, they move beyond that. They *create* Gamesmen. Gamesmen with new Talents, powerful Talents. Peter is one. He is no ordinary Gamesman, no ordinary Talent! I, too, once thought him dead, or as good as! I was wrong. You are wrong now."

Shear interrupted, his mouth full of wine and crumbs which exploded into a little shower upon his black dress. "We do not like being called 'magicians,' Huld. The ignorant Gamesmen may do so, but we expect more courtesy from you. We respect your warnings, but if this Peter is dead, surely . . ."

"You fools, don't you understand? He isn't dead. I don't care what your Gifter said or pretended. Peter is not dead. . . ."

Manacle now, chilly as winter. "I do not appreciate being called a fool. As a direct descendent, unto the thirtieth generation, of the original Searchers, as fifth in a direct line to win the title of Dean, I am not one to be lightly called fool. We bear with you, Huld, though you are a mere Gamesman, because you have been useful. We do not bear with insult, however."

I heard Huld's teeth grind together. To be called a "mere Gamesman" would have been enough. To hear the scorn in Manacle's voice was more than enough.

"You bear with me, *Dean* Manacle, because I am the only one who can warn you of what the Council plots against you, what the Council intends. Without me, you are at the mercy of that strange people, not a tender mercy, Manacle. Now, where are they? Where are the Wizard and the Seer?"

Manacle drew himself up with a trembling hauteur, pompously waving the hovering servitor away. "They are in the laboratories, Huld. I will take you there tonight, after the meeting. You may see for yourself. I will tell you then what the Committee has decided about your request, your request to have access to our defenders. I do not think they will be sympathetic, Huld. They believe that the Council and the Committee are effective counterweights to one another. They believe it is so we keep the world in balance."

"Until the Council grows tired of balance." It was said very quietly, but with enormous menace. With that utterance the room became perfectly still. One of the little girls whimpered, the sound falling into quiet as a pebble into a pool, the ripples spreading ever wider to rebound from the walls, an astonishment of sound. Manacle stared at Huld with eyes grown suddenly wary.

"Why would they wish to destroy the historic balance?" he quavered.

"Why would they not? They grow proud, powerful. They

long for new things. Why else would they have created this 'Peter,' this new Talent? For what other purpose than to change the balance?''

One of the magicians who had stood silent during this exchange, one taller than most, with a face the color of ash, said, ''Do you know this to be true?''

''Professor Quench, I know it almost surely. The likelihood disturbs me greatly. And it should disturb you.''

''We must know,'' said Quench in a voice of lava, flowing, hardening, roughening the room with its splash and flow. ''We must know, Manacle. We must know, Shear. Likely isn't good enough. We must know.''

Manacle dithered, shifted his feet, picked at an invisible spot of lint. ''The Committee of the Faculty,'' he offered, ''the subject is to be brought before the Committee when it meets tonight.''

Quench stared him long in the face, then nodded. ''See that it is,'' he said, walking out of the room, voice splattering behind him. ''See that it is. I will be there.''

Manacle now very much on his dignity, feeling diminished by ashy Quench and burning Huld, flutters at Shear. ''Take the consecrated monsters away, Shear. This has quite disordered my day. If we are to have questions raised like this, out of order, before the Committee has had a chance to consider, well. I have much to prepare.'' He bustled away in the direction Quench had gone. Shear herded the girls away, and my last glimpse of Huld was of his fiery eyes watching Manacle to the end of sight. We went, Mavin and I, quiet as bunwits, down the carpeted hallway and into the place designated. There were pallets there for sleeping, and spigots for a kind of gruel, and a pool for bathing. There was nothing of interest save the tall, barred door which led into Manacle's quarters. Once Shear had gone, it would be no trick to shape a finger into a key, to go out and lock the door behind us.

So we did. ''What will he think when he finds two of us gone?'' I whispered to Mavin.

''He will think the two remaining ate the two who are missing,'' she snarled at me. ''Don't be a fool, boy. Leave the door open as though Shear forgot to lock it. Then he may wonder where his breeders are, but he will not suspect a spy in his own place.''

Shamefaced, I went back to unlock the door. Inside the room the two little girls had settled upon one of the pallets and were engaged in a game of a curious kind. I turned my face away, flushing. Evidently they were not totally mindless. They had been trained to do at least one thing. ''What now?'' I asked Mavin.

''Now I need to think,'' she rasped. I could not understand her anger until she spoke again. ''What is he up to, that fustigar-vomit? What does he mean saying you were created by the Council? I know better than he how you were created, and it was in the usual way. No Council had part in it save the counsel between man and woman. He seeks to trick these magicians in some way for some reason. What is the reason?

''Who are these people, these magicians who do not like to be called magicians? They say they are 'faculty' of a 'college.' Well, I know what a college is. It is only another word for school. Windlow had a college. So did Mertyn. What are faculty except schoolmasters. Hm? Except these seem strangely preoccupied with signs and rituals, speaking often of signtists and Searchers. Is this some kind of religion? Manacle claims himself descended from original Searchers. Well enough. Searchers after what? They hold Gamesmen in contempt. There are no women among them. They seem to admit only four kinds of beings: themselves, monsters, Gamesmen, and pawns. . . .''

''Tallmen,'' I offered.

''Only a lesser kind of monster, or perhaps I should say a superior kind of monster. What is this Council that Huld uses to frighten them with, as a nursemaid uses night-bogies to frighten naughty children?''

''Himaggery spoke of a Council. I thought he said it was a group of very powerful Gamesmen—I think he said Gamesmen. They search out heresy. . . .''

''Some such group has been rumored, yes. But is it that group which Huld speaks of? And meantime we know nothing about Himaggery and Windlow except that they are 'in the laboratories.' Where are the 'laboratories'? What are they? We are rattling around in here like seeds in a dry gourd, making a slithering noise with no sense. Come, son, set a plan for us.''

To hear Mavin say this in such noise and frustration amused
me. There was no time to be amused, no time to treasure that
moment, but I stored it away to gloat over later. Of such moments are adulthood made. I almost said ''manhood,'' but
thought better of that. ''We must not be misled by the puzzle,''
I told her. ''Whatever the Council is, whatever this place
may be, whatever the history of the place or its reasons for
existence—none of these are more important than Himaggery
and Windlow. Manacle will meet Huld after tonight's meeting.
So we will go to the meeting and hear what is said. After that we
will follow Manacle to his meeting with Huld, and Didir must
protect me as best she can. If we are inconspicuous, we will
likely pass unnoticed.'' When I said the word, inconspicuous, it
made me think of Chance, and for a moment I was overcome
with a terrible homesickness for him, for Schooltown, for the
known and familiar and sure. I gasped, but Mavin had not
noticed.

''I will be inconspicuous,'' she growled. ''And I will be patient, but this place itches me.''

It itched me, too, as I tried to find the place of the meeting.
No mind I sought through knew of the meeting or where it might
be held. ''An exclusive group,'' murmured Mavin, when I told
her this. ''Do you suppose the room is never cleaned?''

This took me a moment to puzzle out. Then I understood that
the room would undoubtedly be cleaned by someone, a pawn. I
began to search among pawnish minds, Didir dipping here and
there as we moved above the place. On the sixth or seventh try,
we found a mind which had once known of the place. We went
to it. All of this had taken so much time that we were there only
a moment before the magicians began to arrive, only time to
find a dark corner in a kind of balcony over the main room
where two additional chair-like shapes would go unnoticed. The
place was under a duct which brought in heat, and Mavin settled
into it with a tired sigh.

''One more shift and I would have started to eat myself,'' she
confessed. ''I cannot store as you do, my son.''

I realized with some guilt that Shattnir had gone on storing
power for me at every opportunity. It had begun to feel as natu-

ral as breathing. I let power bleed between us. "Take from me," I whispered to her. "I feel we will not move from this place for some time."

One wall of the place below was made up of hundreds of tiny windows, blank and black, except that on one or two a light crawled wormlike and green. One end of the long table had a slanted surface with buttons and knobs on it. There had been many surfaces like that in this place, controls for the contrivances of the magicians. Both the windows and the control surface looked dusty, unused. A side wall held rows of portraits, face after face, mushroom pale above black garb, gold plates identifying each in letters too small for me to read. The last portrait in the bottom row was of Manacle, however, which told us enough. The tops of the higher frames were black with dust. The carpet of the place was worn through in spots. At each chair was set an empty bottle and a drinking glass, a pad of yellowed paper and a writing implement. At one place the writing implement had been shifted in position, and I could see a pale pattern of it where it had once lain upon the paper. Whoever might once have cleaned the place had not done so recently, perhaps not for years. Dust lay upon everything in a thick, gray film.

Quench came in to sit at the place where the writing implement had been moved. He moved it back onto its shadow, carefully, centering it upon its image before settling into the chair, arms folded across his wide torso. The lines of his boxlike hat seemed to continue downward through his head, obdurately square.

Others entered. There were whispers, mumbling conversations. I risked a questing thought to get pictures of long, half ruined corridors, tumbled portals far to the north and south, ramified networks of dusty catacombs, buried in decay. One of those who entered had white tabs at his throat. Others bowed toward him, murmured "Rector." Time passed. Some fifty were assembled before Manacle entered. Well, now we would learn what we would learn.

"Evening, gentlemen. Evening. Glad to see everyone is here so promptly. Well, we have a considerable agenda this evening. Let's call the meeting to order and get started. Will the Rector give the invocation."

The tab-fronted one rose, stared upward and intoned, "Oh, Lord, we your children have pursued your purposes for thirty generations upon this planet. For a thousand years we have been faithful to your commandments. We have watched the monsters in this place, have kept ourselves separated from them, have kept your sacred ordinances to research and record everything that the monsters do. Now, as we approach the holy season of Contact With Home, be with us as we consider grave matters which are brought before us. Let us be mindful of your ordinances as we consecrate monsters to our use in order that your will may be continued unto future generations. Keep us safe from the vile seducements of Gamesmen and the connivances of the Council. We ask this as faithful sons. Amen."

During this pronouncement, the others in the room had peered restlessly about themselves as though someone else were expected to enter, but no one did. There was a brief silence when the man finished speaking. Manacle sat in his chair with head forward, as though he were asleep. Quench cleared his throat with a hacking noise, and Dean Manacle jerked upright.

"Hmmm," he mumbled. "We will move to the minutes of the last meeting." He rose and pushed one of the buttons on the table before him, saying as he did so, "I am Manacle of Monsters, son of Scythe of Sinners, Dean of the Executive Committee of the Faculty of the College of Searchers. Will Central Control please read the minutes of the last meeting." He tilted his head to one side and seemed to be counting. Around the room the others stared at their fingers or murmured to one another, bored. When a slow count of fifty had passed, Manacle went on, "Since Central Control does not think it necessary to read the minutes of the last meeting, may I have a motion to approve them as unread."

"So move," said Quench. He did not move, however, which was confusing. Again, I knew it must be ritual.

"Seconded," said an anonymous voice from the end of the long table.

"It has been moved by Professor Quench, seconded by Professor Musclejaw, that we approve the minutes of the last meeting as unread. All those in favor . . ." A chorus of grunts and snarls greeted this. "Opposed? Hearing none the motion is passed." There was a pause while Dean Manacle collected himself and shuffled through the papers before him. "We shall move to subcommittee reports . . . the subcommittee on portal repair . . ."

"Nonsense," said Quench.

"I beg your pardon." Manacle looked up, bristling. "The agenda calls for . . ."

"Nonsense. The agenda calls for nonsense. Stupidity. Obtuseness. Obfuscation. Let's talk about the Council. Let's talk about this Gamesman, Huld, who wants access to the defenders!"

Grunts of surprise, voices raised in anger. "The defenders? We don't allow access to the defenders! What did he say?"

"We will have the report on portal repair," Manacle shouted. "And the report on the problems at the monster labs, and on the food stocks brought in by Gifters. These are important matters, Quench. Vital matters . . ."

"How vital?" boomed Quench. "If the Council is planning to destroy us all, how vital is it that the monster labs shall or shall not meet quota? If we are all killed, how important that the northern portal cannot be repaired, as we know it cannot, as the southern portal could not in its time. If there are none left to have appetite, how vital is it that the Gifters bring in their full cargoes of grain and meat? Vital? Manacle, you're a fool and your father before you was a fool."

I had not seen until then the little hammer which Manacle picked up from before him. He whapped it upon the table, raising a cloud of dust at which several members began to sneeze and wipe their eyes. If this was meant to restore order, it failed its purpose. A trembling oldster was shouting at Quench who was bellowing in reply. Elsewhere in the room confusion multiplied as small groups and individuals rose in gesticulating argument. Manacle thrashed with his little hammer, voices rose, until at last Quench shouted down all who would have opposed him.

"Sit down, you blasted idiots. Now you all listen to me for a while. If you choose to do nothing after I've spoken, well, it will be no less than you've done about anything for fifty years. I will speak. I'm a full professor, entitled to my position, and I will be heard, though I am a doddering Emeritus.

"Most of you in this room recall the meeting a generation ago

when Dean Scythe admitted to this Committee that the techs
could not repair the portal machines, or the air machines, or
most of the others, so far as that goes. You recall that we had before us at that time a suggestion, made by me, that we set some
of our brighter young men to studying the old machines and the
old books in order to learn about them. You recall that my suggestion was met with typical revulsion and obstinate lack of understanding. No, you all said, we wouldn't deny our sons their
chance at earning their degrees by asking them to be mere
techs.'' Quench spat the word at them bitterly. ''Oh, no. Every
one of us had been assistant, associate, tutor, lecturer, assistant
professor—all of it. Each of you wanted the same for his boys.
So, old Scythe suggested we pick some *Gamesmen* and bring
them in to learn about the machines, that we give some
Gamesmen the old books, that we turn our future over to the
Gamesmen because we were too proud to be techs. So we
brought some of them in. There was that fellow Nitch, came and
went for a decade. Where is he now? Gone to use what he learned
for his own profit, I have no doubt. And there were others.
Fixed a few things, but not for long. Now there's this fellow
Huld, threatening us with the Council. Telling us the Council is
going to destroy us—the Council we've cooperated with for
hundreds of years by taking up dangerous Gamesmen and putting them away when the Council told us to. Now here's Huld
telling us the Council is *creating* Gamesmen with dangerous
new talents. Here's Huld saying *he* will protect us if we only
give him access to the defenders. And idiot Manacle has half
told him we'd do it. And, while all that's going on, Manacle
wants us to sit here talking about repairing the north portal
which has been in ruins for five generations. Outrageous piffle!'' He subsided into seething silence, picked up the writing
implement before him and broke it in two. There was a horrified
gasp from others in the room.

''You broke the pencil.'' Manacle trembled. ''They've been
here since my great-grandfather's time, and you broke
one. . . .''

''Piffle,'' repeated Quench. The angry silence was not broken until an old voice quavered in treble confusion.

''Excuse me, but what are you suggesting, Professor
Quench? Are you saying we should not listen to Huld? Or

should listen to Huld? Do we now distrust our colleagues of the Council . . .?''

''I'm suggesting,'' said Quench, ''that we do now what we should have done generations ago. Get some of the young assistants and associates out of the watching labs. Let them put their 'search' aside for the moment. There's nothing new in it anyway. Hasn't been anything new in it for ten generations. We can create monsters until we're sick of it and watch them till we're bored to death, and there'll be nothing new in it. Why, a year's watch doesn't produce a footnote. No, let's create a degree in machinery, for College's sake. Create a degree in repair. Let the young men 'search' in the old books. Stop depending upon these Gamesmen . . .''

''Heresy,'' thundered the Rector. ''Professor Quench, you speak heresy of the most pernicious sort. Our forefathers made a sacred covenant with Home to search and record information about monsters. To think of creating a degree in some other discipline . . .''

''Oh, monster offal,'' snarled Quench. ''You pray that we be kept safe from the vile seducements of the Gamesmen, and then you fall right into their vile seducements yourself.''

''Holy Scripture . . .''

''Holy Scripture be shat upon. You read it your way, Rector, and I'll read it mine. When we're all dead, what will be the sense of Holy Scripture? You know what I think of your sacred covenants? They don't make sense!''

''Sir, you question the very basis of our history, the foundations of our faith. . . .''

''I question your data, Rector.'' There was a shocked intake of breath. This was evidently a serious charge, though I could not tell why. ''I question whether our forefathers ever agreed to do what you say they did. In any case, it's susceptible of proof. Ask Home.''

The shocked silence extended, built, was broken at last by Manacle. ''Ask Home? What do you mean, sir?''

''I mean, ask Home. Two days now, isn't it? Aren't we getting the blues assembled for the ceremony? Getting ready for the rigamarole? Going to send the Signal? Right? Signal says we're all spandy-dandy, doing well, following the sacred covenants, right? This time let's tell them we've got some religious

questions and would appreciate çlarification of the scriptures."
He glared at the open mouths around the table. "I dare you.
And, while we're at it, it might be a good idea to find out if the
defenders still work. Lord knows the portals don't."

"The defenders are self-repairing," said Manacle. "If the
Council were to strike at us for any reason, it would be at their
peril. I would release the defenders in a moment, Quench, and
they would work as they did a thousand years ago. Depend upon
it."

"I don't depend upon it," he replied. "I depend upon rust
and decay, spoilation and corrosion, that's what I depend upon.
And on my memory. I remember that we need food and fuel
from outside. There are Gamesmen out there who would limit
our access to those, and the Council has helped us with that by
identifying the rogues and removing them, sending them in to
us to be made into blues. In return, we supply drugs to make
them live long. Balance, Manacle. Balance. Mutual advantage.
Why would they change all that? I think this Gamesman of
yours may be full of vile seducements, all right, and the evil in-
tentions may not come from the Council!"

The Rector, sneering, said, "Does our respected Professor
Emeritus postulate a fifth force? Some mythological concept?"

"Maybe," replied Quench, with a sneer of his own. "Have
you heard of Wizards, Rector? Not your field, hmmm? Haven't
heard of Immutables, either, I suppose? Not your field? No, I
thought not. Well, an aged Emeritus can prowl around outside a
little, as I have done—no, no, don't look horrified—I said I can
prowl around out there without compromising my academic
dignity, even if it isn't my field. There may be a fifth force,
Rector. And I'd like to move we find out . . . ."

"You're out of order." Manacle hammered, raising another
cloud of dust with every blow. "The Agenda says . . ."

"Get your head out of your backside, Manacle! I move we
get some of the young men working on the old books, if they
have wits enough. . . ."

"Is there a second? Motion dies for lack of a second," gabbled Manacle, his voice a shriek which cut through the babble
around him. "I will appoint a subcommittee to study the matter
which the Gamesman Huld has warned us of. Is there further
business to be brought before this committee; hearing none this

meeting is adjourned.'' He collapsed momentarily into his chair, lips moving in and out like a fish's.

"Piffle," shouted Quench. "There's no hope for you."

Mavin and I did not move. There seemed little hope for us either. We had understood hardly a word of what had been said, and below us in the meeting room, Manacle rose and fled through the door as though to escape Quench's words.

10

The Labs

"Don't let Manacle out of our sight," Mavin whispered as we slithered out of our chair shapes and into the guise of ubiquitous, invisible Tallmen. Her warning came late, for we had already lost sight of him, and it was only the sound of his voice echoing back from a twisting corridor which led us in the right direction. He had been joined by Shear, who was receiving a Manacle harangue with obsequious little cries of outrage and acclaim.

"You know why he does it!" asserted Manacle, beating Shear upon the shoulder to emphasize his point. "That Quench! He does it because he never begot a son on his breeders, not one. Only monsters. Dozens of them. Why, the pits are full of his get, but not one boy to carry on the academic tradition. Why should he care whether our boys get their professorships? Not him! 'Get the boys out of the monster labs. Create a degree in machinery,' " he mimicked viciously. "Emeritus or not, he ought to be stripped of his membership on the Committee. He ought to be driven off the Faculty. . . ."

"He has some followers," Shear said nervously. "Some who believe he may be right."

"*Right*? The man's a fool. Wants us to turn out the only person who's capable of helping us. Wants us to send Huld away empty-handed. Scared to death Huld will learn something that will endanger us. Poof. I could give Huld the keys to the defenders this minute, and it wouldn't hurt us as much as making an enemy of him. Well, I have no intention of sending Huld away in a fury. Quench can blather all he likes, but I think we need the man, and I'll tell him how highly we regard him when we meet him. . . ."

"You're meeting Huld?" Shear stared guiltily about, afraid he might be seen. His eyes slid across Mavin and me, but we did not exist in his vision. "Do you think that's wise?"

"I wouldn't do it otherwise," snarled Manacle. "I've had enough, Shear, now don't you start on me. Just trot along here to the labs where I'm meeting Huld and we'll have a talk. My son, Flogshoulder, is supervisor of the transformation labs this term. We'll have privacy, and you can watch them make the blues. That always amuses you."

"Yes. But should Huld see that? I mean, it's private . . . part of the ritual . . ."

"Oh, poof. I know it's part of the ritual, but what does Huld care about that? He knows, in any case. What's he going to do? Steal the bodies?"

I stole a glance at Mavin to find her watching me, puzzlement meeting puzzlement. "What are blues?" I whispered. She crossed her eyes at me in answer.

It was not far to the anteroom where Huld waited, a glossy, much used area beside a high transparent wall. We stared at the place beyond that wall, a lofty area of tall glittering machines, lights which spun and danced, wormcrawls of green light upon a hundred black screens. Green-clad figures moved in this exotic milieu with strange devices in their hands or clamped upon their heads, or both. Manacle greeted Huld, took him by the arm, and tapped upon the glass wall to attract the attention of one of those inside. That one bowed and came to slide a portion of the wall aside.

"Dean Manacle," he said.

"Now, now, no formality, my boy. You've met our good friend, Huld? Huld, my son, Tutor Flogshoulder. He is supervisor of the term here in the transformation labs. You wanted to see the cargo for yourself? Well, Flogshoulder will be glad to take us through and explain the process. If it's convenient, my dear boy."

The dear boy, who suffered from an unfortunate superfluity of teeth, gaped, then covered this gaucherie with a self-conscious giggle. "Oh, it's quite convenient, Father. Most in-

teresting for guests, too. Just come through here. Don't mind
the techs, they haven't the wits of a bunwit and don't understand
anything but machines. . . .'' He led the way into the polished
room, Mavin and I following. I believed they would stop us, see
us, forbid us entry. They did not. Across the room a pair of
Tallmen pushed brooms along the aisles, as invisible as we.

At the first sight of Huld, I had gone deep into myself and
now was letting Didir guide me by small promptings from within as the words of those in the room flowed through and away.
The sight of the two bodies upon the chill dark slab at the center
of the place almost broke my composure. Mavin's was destroyed. I saw her stumble and turn pale before catching herself,
to continue the endless recitation of some nonsense rhyme. The
bodies were Windlow and Himaggery, cold and gray as when I
had seen Windlow at the Blot. I let Didir tune my eyes to their
keenest and watched, to see the slow, slow rise of chests over
the shallowest of breaths. They were alive, alive but laid out
like meat on that dark slab.

Huld approached the slab and hung over the bodies like some
predatory bird, his nose stabbing at them beakwise, peering and
peering until he was satisfied and returned to Manacle's side.

"So, you have two of them," he said. "If you had the boy, I
would have cheered you, Manacle. As it is, you have only de-
layed the time of ruin, not forestalled it.''

"Oh, come, come, my dear fellow. The situation is not that
grave.''

"Grave enough. If you are not to perish with all your colleagues, measures must be taken. Still, having these two is better than nothing. What do you do with them now?''

"We're getting ready for the ceremony, dear fellow. We'll
use these to make blues and bodies for the occasion, two
bunwits with one arrow, so they say. That will remove the threat
of these two, permanently, just as it has removed the threat of
thousands in the past, and it will give us trade goods for the
Gifters. Would you like to see the process?''

I do not know why Mavin and I did not act then. Surely we
did not understand what was to occur, or we did not realize it
would happen at once. Perhaps we had concentrated so on being
unseen and unnoticed that we had not allowed for the need for
sudden intervention. In any case, we did nothing. Flogshoulder

gestured imperiously at one of the greenclad "techs." That man leaned forward to move a long, silver lever. At that the dark slab rotated, dropped, and moved beneath a contorted mass of metal and glass with wires and tubes protruding from it which had been making a low humming sound. The hum ascended into a scream; lights flickered; there was a smell of burning and a cloud of acrid smoke. One of the techs coughed, shouted, pumped a piece of equipment to produce a puff of bad smelling mist. The fire went out; the scream dropped into a hum once more; the slab twisted and returned to its former position.

Himaggery and Windlow were still there, still there, but I knew before Manacle reached forward to tap old Windlow's arm what sound I would hear—the sound of ice, faintly ringing, bell-like, metallic, dead. Beside each frozen skull rested a Gamespiece, tiny, blue. I looked upon them with my Shifter's eyes, eyes which can be those of a hawk to see the beetle upon the grass from a league's height. These "blues" were no crude carvings, no anonymous, featureless gamespieces. These were Himaggery and Windlow in small, each in his appropriate guise, and even the moth wing mask of the Seer could not hide the glitter of Windlow's eyes. If this thing did not weep, I was blind. I started to move forward, but Mavin caught my arm to hold me. If Huld had been alert and Reading at that moment, we would have been discovered. Huld, however, was listening with avid attention to Manacle. If Huld thought the information important, then I did also.

"The contrivance," said Manacle in a pompous, didactic tone which reminded me a little of Gamesmaster Gervaise, "was used by our forefathers when we came to this place. Evidently the length of the journey, or the time it took, did not allow persons to travel while awake and alive in the ordinary way. No, the fleshy part was preserved, as you see, for storage. They can be kept forever, these bodies, or so the techs say. However, when resurrected, these bodies would have no memory, no intelligence—all of that is wiped clean by the process, so we are told. So a record was made. A record containing all thought and memory, and this record was embodied in the form you see. Blues. That is what we call them. We make a few hundred each year to use in the Calling Home ceremony. Then we give them to the Gifters to use in trade. . . ."

"I have seen them," said Huld. "Kept in cold chests. Why are they kept cold?"

"Well—I am not certain. Perhaps one of the techs would know. The techs make the gameboards, after all, don't they Flogshoulder?"

"I will ask a tech, Father. It is not something which interests me. Hardly in our field, you know." He went away to return in a moment with an old, pleat-faced man with tired eyes. "Tech, why are the blues kept in cold chests? And are the gameboards made here? You have a word for it, I think. Micro—micro something?"

"Microcircuitry, Supervisor. The gameboards are made with microcircuitry. To make the Gamespieces move. They are kept cold because they are supposed to last longer that way. The manuals say they break down very rapidly if they get warm."

"There are manuals?" Huld, greedy-voiced. Too greedy-voiced, for Manacle gave him a sharp look before taking him by the arm to guide him away. "So. Interesting, isn't it, Huld? And now you need worry about those two no more. Their bodies will be stored in the caves, used in the ceremony, then put into the caves once more and forever. Their blues will go into some Trader's wagon to be given to some Gamesmaster as a giftie. I sometimes wonder if they feel anything, those bodies. They seem very dead."

Huld, pretending a disinterest I knew he did not feel, "How are the bodies and the blues joined together again?"

"Oh, my dear fellow. Who knows? I wouldn't know. We haven't done that in a thousand years. There may be a book about it somewhere, but I doubt the machinery to do it even works. Why would one care?" They went out the way they had come, still chatting, leaving Mavin and me behind, hidden among the sighing machines. When they had put a little distance between them and us, I hissed at her.

"One of us must go after them. One must stay here to see where they put Windlow and Himaggery. Which?"

She thrust me away. "You must go after Huld. I have no Didir to protect my mind, and I cannot keep up this rhyming and jiggy song forever. You go. I will stay. I will meet you in that place they held the meeting, soon as may be. Go!" And I went.

I went in a fever of impatience and anger, anger at myself, at

Huld, at the silly, fatuous Manacle and his idiot son. If we were to save Himaggery and Windlow now, we would have to restore them to wholeness, put their two halves together, body and spirit, and who knew how to do that? The books? What books and where? I was reaching the end of my ability to slink and sly about, the limit of my self-control. It was Didir and Dorn who saved me, who soothed me into sleep like a fretful child and held me there, barely ticking, while they followed Huld, Manacle, Shear and toothy Flogshoulder deeper into the labyrinth while Huld sought information.

"These books, Manacle. The ones which tell about rejoining the bodies. Have you seen them? Read them? What did they say about . . . the blues?"

"I don't recall seeing anything about them in books. But then, I recall what my father said about them. A pattern, he said. The pattern of a personality. Yes. That was well put. The pattern of a personality. In ancient times, of course, the pattern was reunited with the body when both had reached their destination. It is this process we reenact during the ceremony. We don't really *do* it, of course. Some of the younger men act the part of bodies, and we use the blues symbolically. It's only a ritual, but very impressive for all that. But then I've told you all this before."

"Why don't you actually *do* it?" Huld asked. Didir could detect an avidity in this question though the tone of voice was deliberately casual. "That would be even more impressive."

"Why, ah . . . I'm not sure," began Manacle, only to be interrupted by his unfortunate son.

"Because no one knows how, the techs say. The manuals aren't there, not where they belong. Of course, all techs are fools, as we all know, but that's what they say. . . ."

"Do they think the books were lost?" Huld, pursuing. "Or destroyed, perhaps? Or taken away?"

Flogshoulder put on a thoughtful face, marred by the obvious vacancy within his skull. "I should know. Truly I should. I've heard them talking about it often enough. They say Quench asked for the same books, and they've been looking for them. . . ."

"Quench." Manacle turned red, blustering. "Quench!"

"Yes, Father. Quench thinks it was Nitch took the books,

that's it. You remember Nitch? The books have been gone since he went.''

"Went?" asked Huld softly, so softly. "Went?"

"Away. He went away. At least, I think he went away. Didn't he go away, Father?"

Manacle nodded angrily, muttering and counting under his breath as he walked along. "Quench, thirteen fourteen. Damn Quench. Fifteen. Mind his own business, keep to his place. Sixteen. He and Nitch two of a kind, ungrateful wretches. Seventeen. Ah, this is it. The seventeenth door from the corner, on the right. You wanted to see the defenders, Huld. Well, here we are. I'll just find the key here, somewhere, among all these little ones I think. Gracious, haven't looked in here almost since my investiture. Yes. This one.''

The door swung wide. They went through it, leaving it open behind them. I faded into the wall surface, unseen, unheeded. The room was empty save for one of those control surfaces which abounded in the place, this one with a large red lever and five covered keyholes, all bearing legends in archaic letters of a kind I had seen only once before—in that old book which Windlow had so coveted, the one I had found with the Gamesmen of Barish.

"They are self-repairing," said Manacle in a self-important tone. "Requiring no maintenance, no techs, for which we may rejoice. Should we need to activate them, I have only to turn these keys in those holes, five of them. At one time each key was kept by a separate member of the faculty, but upon my investiture, I brought them all together in the interest of efficiency. There are times when ritual must give way to convenience, don't you agree? So, I have only to insert them thus, and thus, and thus, here, and here, turning each one, so. Now, if any of us were to move the lever, the defenders would be activated at once. We will not do that, of course. There is no need. However, I will leave the keys here and turned, just in case. No point in wasting time later, if your warnings, dear Huld, were to prove accurate and immediate.''

"What—ah, what form do the defenders take?" This in Huld's sweetest voice. Peter, who had been Huld's captive in the dungeons of Bannerwell, did not trust that voice.

"I do not recall ever having heard what form the defenders

take. What is that phrase in the ritual, Flogshoulder? You have learned it more recently than I—gracious, I have not thought of that in fifty years. Something about 'Defense of the home, to hold inviolate—' ''

"No, Father. It goes, 'Should they gain power to the extent that the base is threatened, in order that Home be held inviolate the defenders shall be activated that the signtists and searchers be held in glorious memory.' ''

"That's not how I learned it," objected Shear. "I learned it when I was only a boy, before I could read. It went, 'Should their power and extent again threaten the base, the defenders will assure that Home is inviolate through the selfless action of signtists and searchers held forever in glorious memory.' ''

"Glorious memory," said Manacle happily. "I think of that whenever we have the ceremony. The base. That's where the shiptower is, dear Huld, and therefore the ceremony is held there. It's very impressive, quite my favorite occasion. Let me tell you about it.

"We begin by placing a number of the bodies in the shiptower, along with some of the young fellows who play the part. We put some blues there, as well, for verisimilitude. The unloading machines are all polished and garlanded with flowers.

"Then I, as Dean, have the honor to take the part of Capan. I emerge from the shiptower and recite the inspiring words of dedication. All the Faculty is there, of course, down to the least boychild. I recite the words, then I start the unloading machines and they bring out the bodies and the blues. We put the young men into the rejoining machine, together with some blues to make it look real, and they emerge at once, all glowing and eager. Then I give them the Capan gown. This is symbolic, you understand, of our continuation in the academic tradition from the time of Capan to the present. We still wear the Capan gown in his honor. It is moving, my dear Huld, very moving. Then the machines take the rest of the bodies and the blues, the real ones, away to the caverns while Capan (I still have that part, of course) brings a monster out of the ship and puts her in the pit. This is symbolic too. It symbolizes our mission to search the monsters and record everything about them. Everyone cheers.

"Then, I go back in the shiptower and do the 'Calling Home'

or 'Signal Home' as it's sometimes called. I go alone into the shiptower and instruct the instrument to contact Home with our message, then I come out and tell everybody what message has been called Home and what Home said. Everyone gets very choked up at that, and the choir sings, and the techs serve special cake, and we all drink wine. A very happy time, Huld. A very happy time.'' He wiped his eyes on the corner of his robe, looking all at once grave and grandfatherly, eyes full of an old and childlike joy. I wanted to kick him, but he went on in happy ignorance of my intent. ''We give each other gifts, too, in honor of the occasion. I still have some gifts my father gave me, years ago.''

''You bring a monster out of the ship?'' said Huld. ''Does this mean that in that long ago time your forefathers brought the monsters to this place?''

''Oh, yes. Certainly. Our forefathers came. With the monsters. To keep Home inviolate, to watch and record.''

''Gamesmen were here, then, when your forefathers came?''

''Oh, I suppose so, Huld. Yes. They must have been, how else would they be here now? Your people. And the pawns, of course.''

''And the monsters in your pits are the descendents of those your forefathers brought?''

''Oh, no, sir,'' babbled Flogshoulder, eager with his tiny bits of information. ''They do not reproduce at all well, sir. No, many of the monsters in the pits are made in the monster labs. I will be supervisor there, next term. Also, we pay the Gifters to bring some from outside. And some . . . well, some . . .''

''You may say it, my boy,'' said Manacle, still kindly with his nostalgic glow. ''Some are born to our own consecrated monsters, to be reared in special pits and adapted properly for our use. Waste not, want not.'' He made a high pitched little obscenity of laughter.

''Interesting,'' said Huld. ''Very interesting. Well. If you will just show me whatever books there are which describe the defenders, our business may be concluded for a time.''

''Oh, my dear Huld. I thought you understood. There are no manuals for the defenders! Either there never were any, and that may well be the case, or Nitch took them when he went. In any case, it doesn't matter. They are self-repairing, my dear fellow.

You needn't concern yourself about them. If we need them, we have only to press that lever down. Everything else has been done."

I could feel Huld's baffled fury from across the room, feel his heat. "Dean Manacle. What will happen when the lever is thrust down? Do you know?"

"Well, of course. We will be defended. Haven't I said so again and again. Really, Huld, sometimes you are very trying."

Didir and Dorn pushed me deep into the corner, perhaps to avoid touching Huld as he stormed away, followed by the others who were full of twittered commiseration. "Gamesmen!" said Shear. "They have no manners."

"After all our courtesies to him. Well. He was simply furious to see that we didn't need his warnings as much as he had thought we would. Dreadful blow to his ego. Full of pride, that one is. Still. He'll get over it." Manacle, comfortably full of his own view of his world.

In a moment they were gone. Didir let me come to the surface of myself, drove me to the surface of myself like a volcano exploding within me. I saw shattering lights, felt electric burning and shock, heard her voice, loud, "They are wrong, Peter. Wrong. That is not the way it was. I was there. I was there, I know how it was." Bits of her memory fled across my mind.

A babble erupted inside me, Dorn and Trandilar, Wafnor's hearty cheer dimmed in a wild crosstalk which felt like panic, like fury, like fear. Finally Dorn's voice, dark and heavy as velvet, "Turn the keys back, Peter. Turn the keys back and take them away. . . ." only to hear Didir once more, "No! It must be done in a certain order, a certain order or it goes . . ."

I trembled with vertigo, sick, thrust this way and that by those inside me, without balance or direction. I screamed silently, "Stop! Stop!" and the interior babble ceased. Then Didir's voice, thrumming like a tight bowstring, held from panic by her ancient will, "Did you see the order in which the keys were turned, Peter? Did you observe?" At which I laughed. She herself had kept me submerged during all that time. I had only heard what came to my ears. I felt that tight bowstring thrum, thrum, begin to ravel. "Then leave them alone. Can you lock the door into the corridor?" she shrieked at me.

I could do that, and did, before she broke in a shower of fiery sparks which shook every fiber of me, went down every nerve, dropped me to the floor to lie twitching like some maddened or dying thing while I knew what it was that Didir knew. If the lever in that quiet room behind me were pushed down, something huge and horrible would happen—something final and irretrievable. And Didir believed it would happen to all the place we were in, to the corridors, the mountains, caverns, to all the black-clad magicians and their servants, to their monsters, their machines, and perhaps—perhaps to the world as well.

11

Calling Home

I convulsed, there on the floor, thrashing like a fresh-caught fish. If anyone had come by, they would have found me there in my own shape, naked as an egg and helpless as any fledgling. The presence within which had been Didir became a scattered shower of sparkling half-thoughts, fleeting memories; pictures of herself going to this place or that; pictures of someone else I did not know, tall and dark, gold-decked; premonitions of disaster which unmanned me to leave me gasping without ever making connected sense. Then there was a time, long or short, I never knew, of darkness. When I came to myself again it was to feel the hard, cold floor beneath my wet cheek where I had lain in my own drool.

After a little time, I was more or less myself again. I recognized what had happened—panic. Through all the confusion, I found myself wondering how one of the Gamesmen of Barish could feel panic. But then, I told myself, they were more than mere constructs. They had reality, though they had to use my head to express it—a head which was still splitting with an excruciating pain, pain enough to have panicked *me* and shut down all the places which the Gamesmen had occupied. Didir was gone, but so were Dorn and Trandilar, Shattnir and Wafnor. My head felt empty, vacant and echoing. The pain diminished almost at once, and I lay against the door of that dreadful room, frightened and quite alone. I wondered almost hysterically whether they would come back to me again, so felt for Shattnir because she was the one who was hardest, least vulnerable. Nothing. Her figure lay in my fingers like a doll, wooden, slightly chill. Well, there was no time to experiment or wonder. I had no knowledge of the time which had passed. I had to find Mavin, quickly, and tell her what I knew.

Furred-Peter grew a pair of wide, fragile ears upon his head, like those of the shadow people, and fled through the halls listening for any movement. There was no Didir to warn me, and I was vulnerable in those metal corridors. I fled, promptly losing myself in the maze, unable to fish for thoughts to help me locate myself, following this one and that one at a distance until at last I came to a familiar place from which the committee room could be found. I got there, got in—and found it empty. Mavin was not there. Whether she had been there, I could not tell.

I was alone there for a long time, time enough to get hungry, to find my way to a place food was stored for Tallmen, Tallmen who came and went, saying nothing to me in the guise of a Tallman as I also came and went. The food was tasteless stuff, but it sustained me. I slept a time. I strode back and forth through the committee room, looking at the portraits of Deans from ancient times to the present. Perhaps it was my imagination, but they seemed to grow more and more foolish-looking at either end of the time. Some in the middle looked hard and competent—rather like Himaggery. I thought about that for a while, without reaching any conclusions. Then I had a fit of apprehension about Mavin. Had she been caught? Perhaps killed? Was she lying somewhere wounded, waiting for me to rescue her? I cursed the panic which had driven Didir out of my head and tried to get her back. Nothing. The little figure lay in my hand like a stick. Not a quiver. No, perhaps a quiver, but remote. I tried Shattnir once more. Only a far, faint tingling. Well, whether it was something in the Gamesmen or something in myself, I could not tell. My head felt as though it had been struck by lightning. Perhaps there were fibers there which could be temporarily severed, synapses which could be shocked into quiescence. I waited. I walked about. I chewed my fingernails off, grew others and chewed them off as well.

I was about ready to give up and go on searching alone when she arrived, breathless and weary, desperately glad of the food I had hidden in the balcony of that dusty room.

"Lords, Peter, but that was a journey," she said, falling into long silence while she chewed the tasteless food, eyes closed, body swaying with fatigue. "The techs in that place fiddled about for hours, talking among themselves, mostly about old Quench. It seems that ancient firebrand has been preaching revolution and rebellion to the techs, along with his other strange activities. The techs are mere pawns, Peter, brought in here, put in boots, forced to maintain the place. Some of them are clever. They have learned a lot though they are not given the chance to learn enough." She swayed, chewed, sighed.

"At last they put Himaggery and Windlow upon a kind of cart and wheeled it into a corridor where the cart was attached to a train of similar carts, all loaded with bodies and blues and crates of one thing or another. I hid myself on one of the carts, and a group of pawns rode it as well. Most of them are older men. I believe there have been no young techs trained for some time." She stopped to sip some of the bottled water I had found. "Lords, what a journey. We went north and west, I think, though it is hard to say because of the ways the corridors curve and join. Whatever the direction, we went far and long to the place they keep the bodies, distant and high, lying under some great glacier, I think—some source of endless cold. They are stacked there, Peter, thousands of them, piled like wood for the war-ovens. Endless aisles of them. I saw Throsset of Dowes. He was on top of a pile, like a carving. I saw Minery Mindcaster. I knew her when I was a child and she a marvelous, twinned Talent. They drove the carts into a side room and left them, then they all got on the one little machine which had hauled the rest and went away. There was no place on it for me to hide, and they all knew one another." She put her hand on mine, still shaking with cold. "So, I followed them on foot, and became lost, and took endless time to return." I let the food and drink restore her before I told her what I had learned. When I had done, she questioned me.

"What is Huld up to? You knew him. What do you guess?"

"I guess he is up to gaining power," I said. I knew this to be true, though I was not sure what power Huld sought in this strange haunt of magicians who seemingly were not magicians at all but merely bad custodians of ancient skills and knowledge.

"Huld is not content to be merely Demon, merely Gamesman. He has no wish, I think, to be willingly followed. It is power he wants, power over the unwilling. He wants to be worshipped, yes, but out of fear and trembling, not out of beguilement. He had that, through Mandor, and it was something, but not enough for him. Still, that is why he hates me. Because I conquered Mandor and held Huld against his will, even for that little time."

"And he came to this place—how?"

"I think he learned, somehow, how I had been protected in Schooltown, how Mertyn and Nitch had protected me. He could have Read that from me, easy enough, when I was captive there. I think Huld sought Nitch, sought him and found him—perhaps killed him for what he knew. This is only supposition, but I know Huld, and the idea hangs together." Surprisingly, the idea did hang together, though I had not known until that instant that I had figured it out. "So Huld came here, seeking power, and found Manacle."

"And Nitch had taken certain books?"

"Perhaps. And perhaps Huld had not thought to Read Nitch concerning books, so perhaps the books are gone forever."

"Or perhaps they were lost half a thousand years ago."

"Perhaps."

"So there may be nothing we can find to tell us about these defenders, nothing we can find to tell us how to restore Himaggery and Windlow and a thousand, thousand more. . . ."

"About the defenders, I know only what I caught from Didir's mind before she fled me in panic—or, before I drove her out in a panic of my own. She knew of the defenders. Originally there were five keys, kept by five persons, one of whom was . . . someone near to Didir. The reason for this was to prevent the defenders being accidentally released. Now Manacle has unlocked all the bonds. Any one who gets into that room needs only press a lever down, and whatever it is the defenders do will occur. The idea of this drove Didir into panic, the others as well, and it burst my head with them. Now I cannot raise them."

"You locked the door?"

"I locked the door. Manacle has a key. I have no helpful thoughts about that. Let us think of Himaggery and Windlow instead. So far we have failed horribly at everything we tried to do."

She replied with some asperity. "Who would have thought that rescuing them would have entailed putting them back together? It is difficult to go into a place such as this to set someone free if that person is able to walk and think and assist in the process. I have done that, in one Game or another. It is more difficult if the prisoner is unconscious or wounded, and I have played that Game too, in my time. But to have a prisoner who must be reassembled prior to rescue denies logic and sets all sense awry. I did, however, try to make our process somewhat simpler. I have half of them with me." And she reached into some interior pocket to bring forth the two blues, Himaggery the Wizard, Windlow the Seer, tiny and impeccable, cold and hard. They were only patterns, as Manacle had said. Patterns of personality. Mavin waved at me to keep them, saying, "I have been thinking all the way back how we might put them together again. It may be that the machine used to separate them is the same machine used to reassemble them. In which case, we need only bring the bodies to that laboratory place."

I remembered something Manacle had said. "We need not do that. The bodies are to be brought to a machine, Mavin. Not to the laboratory, but to the 'base' where the ceremony is held. There will be a machine there, too. They will pretend to use it to restore those who play the part of voyagers. The ship thing is there. Manacle called it a shiptower. At any rate, the bodies will be brought there, and there we should be waiting for them."

When she asked me where that might be, I shook my head. I could not use Didir to fish for answers. We knew that Manacle would go there, however, and he was easy enough to find—we knew where his quarters were. "Manacle," commented Mavin, as we went toward his rooms. "The techs hate Manacle. I think some kind of mutiny brews there, my son, an old mutiny."

I thought of Laggy Nap and his power over the boots. "Perhaps the contrivance which controls the boots has fallen into disrepair. Perhaps, if techs are expected to repair things and techs are also controlled by the boots, they have found a way to disrepair it.''

''As I said,'' she murmured, ''mutiny. Something brews.''

Though I had not seen Huld since he had stormed away from us outside the room of the defenders, I felt his presence still like a weight upon my lungs. Without Didir to protect me, I had to be more sly and secretive then heretofore. Thus, it took a sneaking time to come to Manacle's place and hear his rumbling whine through the open door. Shear came out, then went in again, several times. Flogshoulder, too, went in and out, bearing garments of some ceremonial type. They emerged together to go to a dining place, from which we later stole food which was of better quality than that given to Tallmen.

''How long until this ceremony?'' I muttered. ''How long must we lurk in this way?''

''We are so far underground time is without meaning,'' she said. ''Nonetheless, if Manacle said 'two days' when we came into this place, then it cannot be long now. We have blundered about in here for the better part of two days at least. Time grows short, and I am glad of it. I could not bear much more of this.''

I felt it, too, the being without sunlight, without passage of day and night. I wondered if this was how ghosts felt in the grave, separated not only from life but from time as well. This led to other thoughts of gloom and destruction, from which Mavin had to rouse me when Manacle came from his quarters for the final time.

We had no doubt he came out prepared for ceremony. There were stripes of gold upon his sleeves and his high square cap was splattered with gold as well. Shear and Flogshoulder came behind, also decorated, and we went in procession down and down corridors toward a distant gate. It was truly down, as though toward a valley, and it was into a valley we came to see the first light of dawn rouging the heights before us, brightening the cliffs with morning while the forests lay still in night below. Here was a green meadow crisscrossed with metal tracks, heaped with mounds of wrack and jetsam (or so they appeared), with a blackened tower standing at its center, silvered at its tip. A tiny opening gaped high in the side of the tower, like a missing tooth, and a tall spidery ladder stood beneath it. Upon the valley floor small groups of techs removed covers from machines which had been covered against the depredations of time and weather. Near the tower was a machine similar in every respect to that one which had so changed Himaggery and Windlow.

"The blues," whispered Mavin. "See, they are carrying the blues into the tower."

She was right. Some of the techs were carrying boxes of the blues to the tower where a lower section had been opened into some large cargo space. There were no Tallmen on the field. We would have to take the form of techs, and I looked at them closely with my Shifter's eyes before fading back into the shadows to take their shape. Even as we emerged onto the field, the wagons of bodies came out of the tunnels to clatter their way toward the tower. We went purposefully after it, looking neither right nor left, intent upon our pawnish, techish duties.

When we arrived at the tower, we began helping with the loading. Mavin went up into that cargo space, then I. We lifted body after body into it, stacking them, within moments ceasing to think of them as bodies at all. They were only things. When the tech outside put Windlow's feet into my hands for a moment I forgot what I was doing. Mavin brought me to myself.

"Here, pass him to me. I have found a place to hide them."

So then I did double duty while she dragged Windlow away somewhere, then Himaggery, when he emerged from the general pile.

When the tech outside thrust up the last body to me where I stood inside the tower, he said, "Those who follow Quench, in the southeast portal, as soon as the ceremony starts . . ." then turned away from me as though he had not spoken, waiting for no answer. I had sense enough to step back out of the light. When I turned, Mavin was there, nodding.

"I heard him," she said. "I told you, Peter. Mutiny. It will happen during the ceremony, when all the magicians are here. Mark me, it will happen. Now come see where I have put them."

The tower seemed small from outside, but from within it was a warren of twisting halls and tiny cubbies, many no bigger than closets, with mattressed shelves which were obviously beds. So it was a ship. A ship. How could it be? I turned to Mavin with the question on my lips.

"Not a water-going ship, Peter. Think! Put together the pieces. You spent long enough with Himaggery to have learned to do that. . . ."

She showed me where she had put them, in one of the little cubbies, half hidden behind a huge pipe which seemed to run the entire height of the place, from tip to base. At that moment I wanted only to lie down beside the cold bodies and sleep, but she dragged me around the pipe and into it, where stairs wound up and up to some dizzying termination.

"We need to find a place to watch from," she said, dragging me along behind her. So we went, up and up, coming at last to that open place we had seen from the tunnel mouth. The spidery stairs were just outside. Far below on the grass the magicians were assembling.

Now, how can I make you see what we saw, Mavin and I? I must, for in what we saw was much of old Windlow's conjecture and Himaggery's purpose, much of my confusion and Mavin's effort. It was in that ceremony we learned what we were, and why, and I, all unwitting of what was to come, was only sleepy, lonely, and a little afraid of what might happen at any time. So let me step outside of that and tell you what you would have seen, had you been there.

On a grassy hill were rows of the young magicians, ordered inexplicably by one who stood before them, each holding a book before him. Here and there upon the grass groups of the magicians stood about, chatting with one another. The sun came down, lighting all with a kind of innocent glory. The young magicians began to sing. I had never heard music like that before. It soared and pierced, made me want to laugh and cry. Some of the voices were as high, almost, as women's voices, others a rumbling bass, muttering like drums. I had thought these magicians wholly without honor or sense. Now I had to revise my opinion. Whatever they lacked, they did not lack art. Perhaps it was this art that had kept them alive. I looked down from my high perch to see Manacle at the foot of the ladder, the tears flowing down his face, a face lit from within with a kind of exaltation.

After the singing came a blare of trumpets. This came from a machine somewhere. The sound was inglorious compared to what had gone before. Manacle came up the ladder, slowly, puffing a little as he climbed. Below him the groups of magicians drew away to seat themselves. I counted them while he climbed, perhaps a thousand. Not many to rattle in a place of such size. Of that thousand, there were only fifty or sixty young ones, and one or two were very young indeed, being carried by their fathers who pointed out each step of the ceremony.

Mavin and I took the shapes of the place around us, were invisible when Manacle stepped from the high ladder into the tower. Once there he closed the door behind him, then waited for some signal from without. It came in a second blare of trumpets, and a hideous, monstrous machine-like roaring which built into an unbearable level of sound before fading away. I heard Manacle murmur, ''The sound of the ship landing. Now. The ship has landed.'' He thrust the door before him open and went out onto the ladder.

See it now, this tiny man upon this high place, all in gold-decked black, his fellows gathered below and staring upward, pale faces like saucers there, silence, and respect from every eye. Hear him cry out in a voice changed and made dramatic, ''Behold the planet. I, Capan Barish, have brought signtists and Searchers from afar upon a sacred mission. Come forth! Come forth!''

Then see the machines reach into the shiptower and remove the bodies of the young magicians who were playing the part, all covered with paint to appear gray and hard. See the machines take blues from the ship, clatter and clamor across the grass to the great, garlanded resurrection contrivance, decked with flowers and fluttering with ribbons of silver and gold, all dancing in the light wind of morning. See the young magicians laid upon the slab with the blues, from which they leap up, shouting, wiping the paint from their faces as Manacle comes down from his high place, slow step by slow step, all in dignity and purpose to greet each one of them and drop a black gown over each clean-wiped head. Then see them move away across the meadow while the machine goes on unloading, real bodies this time, and Manacle begins his slow climb up the spidery ladder once more. As he climbed, the singing began again, and I found myself wishing he would not climb so fast if the singing might go on while he climbed forever. Silly. Yes, but it was what I thought and what you would have thought had you heard it.

Then was an unexpected interruption. Manacle came through the entry and back into the ship to make inexplicable clicks and bangs, opening and shutting something. In a short time he was back, leading by the hand one of the consecrated monsters. . . .

No. Leading by the hand a young woman. She was naked to the waist, her high breasts tilted and goosefleshed in the chill, her empty face staring outward at nothing. Manacle led her out upon the ladder, crying, "Behold, the monster! Toward which all your Search shall be that Home be kept inviolate!" Then he took her down the stairs to a pit they had prepared for her somewhere below. I did not see that, could not. When he had led her out, I had remembered. They were Didir's memories, burned into me outside that room of the defenders, as real to me as my own. I remembered the landing, the huge sound of the engines, fires guttering blackly at the base of the ship, green hills in early light. I had been half naked, just wakened by Captain, as he had promised, before any of the others. He supported me with one arm, gesturing out at the world, "Behold, little monster. A world for you, and for me, and for our children and our children's children. . . ." And I, Didir, had said, "The researchers will not let us have this world," and he had replied, "Some day . . ."

It had been the sight of the girl's body and the gold-striped uniform which had stormed the old memory, the sound of a male voice, lustful, adoring, confident. It was only a memory, but it collapsed me, and I came to myself with Mavin shaking me, saying, "Peter! What ails you? Come to, boy. Manacle is coming back up the ladder." So, I drew myself together and we hid ourselves once more, fortuitously, as it happened. Before Manacle arrived, someone else came up the hidden stair. Quench.

Quench, scuttering into the place and hiding himself all in one swift motion as though he had practiced it twenty times before. I heard Manacle arriving, heard the singing begin again, slow, ceremonial, mighty and premonitory. Some great climactic thing was to happen now. The music made that clear.

But all that happened was that Manacle shut the door behind

him and sat down, disconsolately, upon the metal floor. He took a writing implement from a pocket, with a piece of paper, and sat there, alternately chewing the one and jotting upon the other.

The singing built into a climax, slowed, and dwindled to silence. Still he sat. After a time the singing began again, and it went as before. At this, he stood up and sighed, murmuring to himself. "Well, well. That will do as well as any message. I used it five years ago, but it will do as well as any." And reached to open the door.

"Do as well as what, Manacle?" It was Quench, leaning against a shiny panel, boring into Manacle with eyes which could have burned holes in stone. "Why have you not Called Home, Manacle? That is what you are supposed to have done. Call Home. I wish to hear what Home has to say!"

"Oh, Quench. Quench, you monster. What are you doing here? Why have you come? You are disrupting the ceremony. Get out of my way. I have to tell them. . . ."

"Tell them what? That you did not Call Home? That there was no message from Home? That there has not been any message from Home for—for how long, Manacle? How long, you little, insignificant dribble. How long?" He shook Manacle, waving him like a flag. "Tell me, or I'll break your bones."

"Don't be a fool, Quench. You know it's only a ceremony. We all know it's only a ceremony. The message from Home is only a ritual. We all know . . ."

"We don't all know. We all may suspect, but we don't all know. How long has it been, Manacle. I *want* to know. Now!"

"My . . . my great-grandfather's time. Not since then. Not since then to Call Home. And no message received from Home long before that. The machines stopped working, Quench. It wasn't anyone's fault. They just stopped working."

"So it's all a mockery and a deceit. All of it. The monster watching, and the Faculty—all of it."

"No, no, Quench. You know that isn't true. It's worth something, worth preserving. You mustn't, mustn't . . ."

"I mustn't, mustn't I? Manacle, for the sake of those poor fools down there, I won't drag you out on the platform and expose you for what you are, an empty sack of nothing. I'll leave you to go to them, Manacle, with your lies and your ceremonial message. You! I remember a time when being Capan meant something. As for me, I'm off to the Council. . . ."

"What—where—what are you going to do?"

"I'm leaving, Manacle. I'm leaving with all the techs who want to leave with me, and that means almost all of them. We disabled the power machine for the boots this morning. You can't hold them, and they won't be held. We're going. Some of the younger men may go with us, and if not—well, be that as it may. I'm sorry for you all, Manacle, but there's nothing I can do to save you, and I won't perish with you."

And he was gone, clattering down the spiralling stairs. Mavin and I could hear him, down and down until the sound faded, and I knew he had come to the cargo space at the bottom and gone out through it. Manacle was crying before us, great tears oozing down his face. The singing outside had reached its climax once more. He gulped, made a little heartbroken sound, then wiped his face upon his sleeve, leaving long red welts upon it from the harsh gold trim. Unconscious of this he stepped to the door, straightened himself, and opened it. As Mavin and I slipped away to follow Quench, we heard his voice crying to the world, "Message, message from Home . . ."

12

Huld Again

We arrived at the cargo space near the bottom of the tower—the "ship"—only moments before Manacle himself came down. He wore a forced, fixed smile as he met Flogshoulder and Shear near the ladder. I heard Shear say, "Where are the techs? They should be here to unload the bodies and take them back to . . ." and Flogshoulder interrupting, as always, with some inconsequentiality. Manacle did not hear either of them.

He laid hands upon Flogshoulder and said, "Quiet, my boy. Be still. Now listen to me, for all your life is worth. Remember the room where we were yesterday? The room which controls the defenders? Good. That's a good boy. Now, I want you to go there. I left it unlocked for you. I want you to press the lever *down*. Just do that, my boy. Then come back and tell me." He patted Flogshoulder, almost absentmindedly, as he turned to Shear with that same fixed smile.

"Shear. There's a minor emergency. Nothing we can't take care of, but I think the Committee should be advised. Can you go among the celebrants and suggest that we move the celebration indoors? Hmm? And tell the Committee members we will meet them in the Committee room. Have you seen Huld? No. Well, that was more than I could hope for, perhaps. . . ."

Shear and Manacle began a slow circling movement among those gathered in the grassy space. I remembered Manacle saying that the techs would serve cakes and wine. There were no techs, and the magicians were looking about themselves with pursed lips and expressions of annoyance. A mutter began, grew in

volume as the celebrants moved away, away toward the doors.
We waited for the last dawdlers to leave before emerging from
the ship with the bodies of Windlow and Himaggery carried before us. We staggered across the grass to the machine. When we
came close, I was horrified to see that the ribbons and garlands
covered areas of corrosion. Wires and tubes appeared fused together into a blackened mass. We stared at each other for a moment. "What can we do but try?" asked Mavin. "We must."

We laid Himaggery upon the slab, placed the tiny blue in the
recess beside his head, and Mavin went to the long, silver lever
which protruded at the side. Her eyes were shut, her lips moving. I don't know whom she invoked, what godling or devil.
Perhaps it was only herself she counseled. Her hands were
steady when she thrust the lever up, in the opposite direction we
had seen it moved in the laboratories, and I knew she had been
thinking of that, puzzling it out. Could it be that simple? I could
not dare to hope it was.

The machine screamed. I bit my lips until the blood came.
The slab moved, turned, swung beneath the blackened mass
which towered above it. I smelled smoke, burning oil. There
was no device here to put out fire. I only held my breath and
waited, waited while the scream rose to an agonized howl before diminishing to silence. The slab had not returned. Mavin
jiggled the lever, once, twice. Slowly the slab dropped from beneath the machine, down, twisting, out and back toward us once
again. The blue was gone. Himaggery looked like Himaggery
once more. I could see his chest move, tiny, tiny movements,
the shallowest of breaths. We pulled him from the slab and put
Windlow in his place.

I knelt above Himaggery while Mavin went to the lever
again. I heard the ascending howl, smelled burning once more.
This time there was smoke, harsh and biting. I coughed.
Himaggery coughed. His head moved, his hand. I found myself
patting him, stroking him, mumbling nonsense into his ear.
Then Mavin's cry from behind me brought me to my feet.

The machine was on fire. Below the contorted mass, the slab
moved out slowly, too slowly. Already I could see that the blue
was still there. Nothing had happened. Then, when it came further into view, I knew that something had happened—
Windlow's body had been . . . changed. Was it the heat of the

machine? Some ancient device which had broken at last, irretrievably? It didn't matter. What lay upon the slab could not support life again, and I knew this with every cell which Dealpas had inhabited. "Dead," I whispered, unable to believe it. "Dead . . ."

"Dead?" The voice behind me was Himaggery's. I turned to see him trying to sit up, failing, and trying once again. His eyes were unfocused, blind. Mavin was beside him in that instant, ready with one of the black dresses which Manacle had used in his ceremony, ready to wrap him and coerce him back into life once more. I reached over the slab and took Windlow's blue into my hands, hands sticky with tears. I tried not to look at the slab again, but could not stop the thought that this, this is what old Windlow had foreseen and begged for my help against.

Perhaps Mavin read my mind, or my face. She snapped at me. "There is no time for guilt, Peter. We must get out of this place. What Didir feared will happen very soon. . . ."

"The door is locked," I said stupidly. "Flogshoulder will find the door locked. He will have to return to get the key. We have a little time."

"We have no time. Didir warned of some general catastrophe. Gamelords know how far we would have to go to escape it, but the farthest, the soonest would be best." She leaned across Himaggery once more, urging him to his feet. I do not know how he did it, but the man lurched upright, mouth open in anguish as he did so. She went on even as she urged him toward the tunnels. "The cars that brought the bodies to this place are still there, still on the track. I watched them when they ran them. They will take us away."

I followed her, placing Windlow's blue tenderly in my pocket as I went. The carts were there, just as she had said. Himaggery and I climbed into the foremost one as Mavin fumbled with the controls. It shuddered, made a grating noise, then began to run forward into the mountains.

"Where?" I asked her, seeing the daylight vanish behind us. "Where will you take us?"

"Where the tracks go," she replied. "The carts came from those cold caverns, they should return there. We need distance between us and this place, and any other way would take too long. . . ."

So we ran off into a half darkness.

There were no magicians. There were no techs. We saw one or two Tallmen from time to time, but they stood by the walls as still and silent as trees, but unalive. It was then I began to know that they had not truly been living things—or not entirely living things. I thought of Tallmen, and I thought of music, and I wondered how those who made the one could make the other. I have not yet made an answer to that.

Somewhere early in the journey, Himaggery began to regain his wits. He wanted to know what had happened, and in order to tell him that I had to tell him everything, Laggy Nap, my journey, Mavin, Izia, the Tallmen, Manacle, Quench . . . and Didir. We passed one of those dining places once, and Mavin stopped while we raided it. After that, Himaggery seemed to be better, though still rather disoriented and weak. When he asked about Windlow, I could not answer him. I could only look back the way we had come and let the tears run down my face. So it was Mavin who told him, and then there was a silence which seemed without end.

Finally he broke it. "So what is happening now?"

"Now we are trying to get away," I answered. "Flog-shoulder will go to the room. He will find it locked. He will return to Manacle, and one way or another, with Committee approval or without it, Manacle will give him the key. Or Manacle will go himself. Whatever occurs, it will not take long. Manacle will believe that Quench is more of a threat than he ever believed the Council was. The defenders are to be used against a threat. So, he will use the defenders."

"What will happen?" whispered Himaggery from a dry throat.

"I don't know for sure. I *believe* that the defenders were never designed to defend the magicians. They were designed to defend Home, wherever that may be. Another world, somewhere."

"So you've figured that out," said Mavin, drily.

"Yes. The defenders were designed to defend Home against the monsters."

"Monsters?" asked Himaggery. "What monsters? Who?"

"Oh, Himaggery." I laughed and cried all at once. "You. Me. Mavin. All the children of Didir. *She* was the monster, the girl monster, the one the ship brought. Only she. And all those others to watch her and write down everything she did. All of it, the defenders, everything. Just to keep one little woman monster from threatening Home.''

"I thought so," said Mavin. "I thought that was the way of it.''

"Well, if you thought so, I wish to heaven you had told me!" I said.

"So what will the defenders do?" Himaggery went on, tenacious as always.

"Destroy the place," said Mavin with finality. "Destroy Manacle and stupid Flogshoulder and sycophantic Shear, all the Tallmen and the pits, all the monsters—the real ones—and machines. Everything. Or so I believe.''

"So do I," I said. "And we had best be far away when that happens.''

"How far away?"

I couldn't tell him. Didir had thought only of danger, danger to everything. She had not limited it to a certain circle, a Demesne which could be measured for chill. "Far," I said. "As far as possible.''

"At least to the end of these tracks," said Mavin, practical as always. So we rode along the tracks, deeper and deeper under the mountains as Himaggery grew stronger and I felt more the pain of Windlow's death. Once I thought of asking Mavin whether there was some way out of the place she was taking us, but decided she would not appreciate the question. If there was a way out, there would be a way out. If not, not. My asking would not change it.

The way to the caverns was a long way. When we arrived there, I wished we had not come. The bodies around us lay in piles as high as my shoulders, five or six bodies high, men and women together, stacked in endless rows. In one area to the side of the entry, Mavin and Himaggery found body after body of those they had known. Here were those Mavin had mentioned to me, but many others as well.

"And all of their minds—their memories, all, gone? Out there? In the aeries of Gamesmasters, to be used as teaching aids for children?" Himaggery sounded unbelieving, but we assured him it was true.

"Then what threatened us and worked against us was not the Council at all? It was these old men in this moldy place? Abducting us one by one and storing us away like fish?" Again we assured him this was true.

"Then we have only to tell the world what has gone on here, and it will stop. The Traders can be watched."

"That may be true," I said. "But there may be more to it than that. It was these old men who abducted and kept you, true. But Quench said it was the Council told them *who* to take and keep. And it is to the Council that Quench has gone, gone with every tech in the place."

"And," said Mavin, "I would wager with every book they could lay hands on."

We had not yet gone into the largest part of the cavern, a place from which a chill wind came to assure us of egress somewhere. It was then, as we were readying ourselves to find it, that the first rumble came, shivering the rock about us and dropping dust and ice onto our heads from far above. The shaking went on. Rock grated and twisted beneath us.

"We have taken too long," shouted Mavin. "Through the large cavern, quickly. . . ."

But we were not allowed to go.

We had no sooner stepped within the large cavern than he came from behind a pile of bodies, Demon helmed, all in silver, a strange device cradled in his arms, its ominous tip pointed toward me. "Peter, the Necromancer," he said. "I told them you were not dead! I would not let you be dead! Not you, Peter. Not until I could do it myself! I call Game, and Move. Necromancer Nine!"

Himaggery leapt to one side, behind a pile of bodies. Well, he was older than I. He had more experience with this kind of thing. On the other side, Mavin Shifted into something quick and fierce, and the corner of my eye saw her fade into an aisle. Well, she, too was a more experienced Shifter than I. I did not move. The tip of the thing which pointed at me said *do not move*, and I understood its language. "What have you there, Huld?" I asked him, almost conversationally. I was not unafraid. I was simply too surprised to act frightened.

"A thing Nitch made for me, Peter. Was that not kind of him? It was when you all thought me bottled up in Bannerwell.

Do not trust Immutables to do your bottling for you, Peter. They do not do it well. They have no skill in foxing or outfoxing; any Gamesman could outwit them, as I did. I had another place to go, a better place. I found Nitch as he traveled between Schooltown and that place of the magicians. Nitch. It was Nitch who was responsible for what happened to Mandor, Peter. Remember that. What happened to him was just.''

"What happened to him?'' I had put one hand into my pocket, feeling desperately for—for what? Shattnir could do me no good in this cold place. Those around me were not dead to be raised by Dorn. And neither would come to me in any case. . . .

"Why, he died,'' he said, pretending surprise. "After he had made me the things I wanted, told me the things I wanted to know, given me the books he had. He made this shield, like the one you had in Schooltown. This weapon, like no other you have ever seen. Oh, Peter, with this weapon there will be no Gaming against Huld. No. All the Gaming will be as *I* choose.'' He stroked the thing exultantly. "After I dispose of your . . . family . . .'' He drew out the word to make it an obscenity. Until that moment, I had not thought of them as my family, but they were. Himaggery. Mavin. My own kind. My fingers still groped in my pocket. Habit, not hope.

And closed around a Gamesman, closed to feel a warm, wonderful certainty rise through me, soft and gentle, kind as summer, the voice whispering as familiar, almost, as my own. "Peter. Why are you standing here? Valor is all well and good, but shouldn't you be elsewhere if you can manage it?''

It was Windlow.

I almost laughed aloud before remembering the threat. Yes, I know that is foolish. It was only an instant thing, as quickly suppressed. I let Windlow go and burrowed deep to close around a figure I had not tried until then. Old as Didir, powerful as she, her mate and coeval, Tamor. Grandfather Tamor. Towering Tamor.

There was no hesitation. The block, whatever it might have been, had been healed. Perhaps Windlow had healed it. Tamor came into me like a hawk stooping, and I was looking down on Huld as he peered at the place I had been. There was no sensation of flying as I had often thought there would be. No, I was simply lying high upon the air, above Huld, seeing Mavin and

Himaggery moving stealthily toward him around barriers of
chill bodies.

"Huld!" I cried.

He pointed the device up, released a bolt of force which blis-
tered past me and melted stone and hanging ice from the arched
ceiling far above. Liquid rock fell past me, hardening as it
came, and Huld ran from the lethal rain even as I swooped away
to another part of the cavern. More stone and ice rained down.
This was no result of Huld's weapon. This was more of the
same quaking we had felt before. Mavin waved to attract my attention, pointed to the far end of the great cavern. I nodded to
show her that I understood.

I should have watched Huld, not Mavin, for another bolt
from the weapon came toward me, touched me agonizingly,
and splashed against the ice. "All right," said Tamor from
within. "Keep your eyes open, boy. Shall we rescue your
friend?" Himaggery did look lonely and lost, sprawled out below me between two piles of bodies. We swooped down, not at
all birdlike, to grab him and lift him high in a long shallow glide
which took us toward the cavern end. I heard Huld screaming in
fury. He had known of some of my Talents. He had not known
of them all. Well, how could he have done? I had not known of
them myself.

"You will not get away," he was screaming at me. "I've
closed that way out. I knew you'd come here, come where the
bodies of your allies lay. I knew you'd try to get them. It's the
kind of Gamish stupidity they taught you, boy. . . .

"Even if you escape, it won't stop me. I'll come after you
again, and yet again. I have allies, too. And plans. And the
world will not hold us both as Masters, so you will serve my
Game. . . ."

"Tchuck." Tamor made a tsking sound in my head. "That
kind of hysterical threat is unbecoming, undignified. I do not
like being called Grandfather to that." We were away on another long, swooping glide that broke twice to escape bolts from
Huld's weapon. A great slab of stone turned red behind us and
slid toward the floor, half flowing. Without thinking, I reached
for Shattnir and felt her run into me like wine, reaching out toward the melted stone to draw its heat and power into every fiber. We stayed there, hidden behind the bodies, until I heard

Huld coming, then rose once more, lying flat, skimming like an arrow behind the stacked bodies toward the chill wind. Himaggery gasped. I was holding him under one Shifted arm, huge and hairy as a pombi's leg. Well, he should have been used to Shifter ways. In order to get me upon my mother he should have known her rather well.

The shaking of the cavern was constant. I heard Huld shout something, away behind me, then another shout which sounded like fear. He had either been under a falling chunk of rock or had been narrowly missed. I didn't care which. The opening of the cavern was before me. Mavin was already there. The entrance was covered by a narrow grill which sizzled with the same force Huld's weapon had used. Mavin spread her hands wide in consternation. She could not Shift to go through the narrow openings without frying herself. Within me, Shattnir laughed. The laughter of Shattnir had nothing of humor in it. It was not an experience, then or thereafter, which I greatly enjoyed.

All the heat of the great melted slab went into the bolt which broke the grill, melted it in its turn, and spread its broken shards over half the mountain side. Mavin fled through the opening, out and down, knowing I would follow. Around us the earth clamored, no longer quivering but heaving to and fro in long, hideous waves. I flew through the opening into nubilous air, high into gray cloud to see the white wings of a huge bird slide through the gloom beneath me.

Then we saw it, Himaggery and I. Away to the southeast, where the shiptower might have been, a ball of flame, swelling, swelling into a little sun, a cloud rising from it lit from below, bloody and skull-shaped in the murk, fires within it, lightnings playing upon its top. The wind took us then, tumbling us over and over in the high air on the face of a hot wind which Shattnir merely sucked into me and stored away. The earth roared, heaved, and fell in mighty undulations. I saw a mountain tremble, throw back its head and laugh into roaring fragments as we spun through the air again, rolling on the wind. Wild fire licked and crackled and eventually died.

After a time we came down, onto a green hill which sat quietly beneath us, steady as a chair. Wind from the north whipped the bloody clouds to tatters and away. The sun broke through, midway down the western sky. It was not a day, yet, since we had hidden in the shiptower to see the Ceremony of Calling Home. Beside me, Himaggery picked up a straw and closed trembling lips upon it.

"Well, lad. What do you think we should do now?"

I picked up a straw of my own.

"I don't know what you want to do, Himaggery," I said. "But I'm going to change myself into a Dragon and go looking for my mother."

13

Bright Demesne

We found Mavin on her pinnacle, just where I had thought she would be, and she was properly admiring of the most splendid Dragon she or anyone in the world had ever seen. It was exactly as Chance had said, a fool idea. The fire and speed and wind in the wings were all very well, but there was still Windlow in my pocket and the bodies of ten thousand great Gamesmen (as well as a few pawns) lying in the cavern under the snows. Oh, we had gone back, Himaggery and I, just to be sure. The cavern was quite intact except for a little fallen ice and melted stone. Huld was not there, dead nor alive, which meant he was still at large in the world, hunting me. I was growing tired of that.

So, once I had done my gomerousing around as a Dragon, I settled with Himaggery and Mavin on the pinnacle, to await the arrival of my cousins. We sat about Mavin's fire, me watching Himaggery be excruciatingly polite to her while she twitted him at every opportunity. I finally took her aside and told her to let him alone. If she truly did not want to be the man's pawnish mate, I told her, then she should not keep saying so so vehemently, which would just make him believe the opposite. I don't know how I figured that out, except that Trandilar probably had something to do with it. At any rate, it bought us some peace and we got along better.

Swolwys and Dolwys arrived in good time. They had delivered Izia, improved in both health and spirits by the time they arrived. More important, when they had come to Izia's home, Yarrel had been there and she had remembered him. The cous-

ins did not say much about that meeting. I hoped for their sakes
that Yarrel had not treated them as coldly as he had treated me
when last we met. His rejection of me still hurt, and I hoped that
Izia's return might make him feel more kindly, though I knew
that if he learned all she had gone through in the intervening
years, he might hate all Gamesmen even more.

And this line of thought brought me to thoughts of Windlow.
I figured that matter out in the privacy of the cave, unwilling to
talk about it with anyone. I simply chipped at the corner of the
tiny Didir figure with my thumbnail until the white covering
flaked away to show the blue beneath. The Gamesmen of Barish
were blues, simply (simply!) blues, made in the long past for
some reason I could not know, though I was beginning to make
some rather astonishing guesses. The Gamesmen themselves
did not tell me, though whether they could not or would not, I
did not know. At the moment I was content to let things be. Except for one thing.

At one time or another, casually, over a period of several
days, I handed one or another of the Gamesmen to my cousins,
to Mavin, even to Himaggery. They handled them as I had
done, with bare hands, but they gave no indication that they felt
anything or experienced anything at all. So. "Blues" could not
be Read by anyone who handled them. It was a particular Talent
which I had, seemingly I alone of all the world. So again. No
one had seen me take the Windlow blue. No one knew I had it. I
doubt that either Mavin or Himaggery ever thought about it, and
I did nothing at all to remind them.

We traveled to the Bright Demesne together, three horses and
two horsemen. We younger ones were the horses, two for riding, one for baggage. I thought of Chance when I did it. He
would have approved mightily of how inconspicuous I was.

I could not help but overhear the long conversations between
my mother and—Himaggery (I could not think of him as "Father"). As the hours of our travel wore on, they spoke more and
more often of certain Gamesmen they had known. I heard again
the name of Throsset of Dowes. I heard again the name of
Minery Mindcaster. Himaggery spoke of the High Wizard
Chamferton, and Bartelmy of the Ban. They were cataloging all
those they had seen in the cavern or suspected might be there.

And they were making plans to bring all the blues of all the world to the Bright Demesne. "There will be a way," Himaggery insisted. "A way to do it without the machines. Or to build a new machine to do it. So many, so great. We cannot leave them there, stacked like stove wood."

And then they would talk more, list more names, and end by saying the same thing again. Peter in the horse's head nodded wisely. We were no sooner out of one mess than we would get into another.

And, of course, they talked about the Council. The mysterious Council. The wonderful Council. The probably threatening Council. They could not decide whether it was totally inimical, perhaps beneficial, or, possibly, nonexistent. Peter inside the horse's head nodded again. Such questions could not be left unanswered, not by one like Himaggery. Peter inside the horse's head had other thoughts, about Quench, Huld, books, about what several hundred or thousand pawns who had been "techs" might do when loosed into a world which did not know they existed.

And we came at last to the Bright Demesne. Word having been sent ahead, we were expected. There was a certain amount of orderly rejoicing, and Mertyn seemed to have some trouble letting me out of his sight for several days. Chance, on the other hand, behaved as though I had only been gone on a day-long mushroom hunt and was no different on my return than on my going. Only the quantity and quality of the food which kept appearing before me told me that he had worried about me. I helped him by pretending I did not notice.

There was mourning, too, for Windlow. I wept with the rest and kept my mouth shut.

And then Izia arrived—with Yarrel.

They rode into the kitchen court about noon. I was in the kitchen garden with Chance, pulling carrots. There is no Talented way to do this easier than simply stooping over and yanking them out by their tops. So I was muddy and sweating and unsuspecting when the clatter of hooves came from the cobbled yard. I looked up, wiping my eyes with my shirttail, and saw Izia looking at me, very pale and very beautiful. She reached one hand to the person beside her, and then I saw Yarrel. He was looking at me, too, but with an expression in which resentment and eagerness seemed equally combined. He slid from the horse's back, helped Izia down, and they came together toward me. All I could think of was that I wanted to hide, not to have him angry or hateful to me again.

Perhaps he saw this emotion on my face, for he stopped and smiled, almost shyly. "Peter . . ."

Was there something of a plea in that voice? I gritted my teeth and stepped forward, the shirttail still between my hands, wiping away the mud so that I could offer him a clean hand. He did not wait for that, but took both muddy fists in his own and drew me within the circle of his arms.

It was only a moment, a moment before he stepped back, his face calm again as he raised his hand to Chance and let me guide them into the kitchens. We sat there in the fireglow as we had sat year on year, within hands' clasp of one another, eating Chance's baking and telling one another of all that had happened in our worlds. It would be good to write that all was as it once had been, the old friendship, the old closeness. But that would be a sentimental story, not true. It was not as it had been; it was only better than it was before he came.

And Izia sat there, sometimes smiling a little, a tiny smile, tight and tentative, but a smile, nonetheless. Once she even laughed, a short little hoot of laughter, like a surprised owl. I knew then that I had loved her for herself, and because she resembled him, and because I had rescued her. I knew in that same way that she would never know it, that it would only be a burden to her. She could accept Yarrel's touch, and only his, a gentling, animal-handler's touch, with nothing in it of lust or human ardor. She would grow more secure, less frightened, as the years went by. But—no, she would never accept what might remind her of Laggy Nap. Nap. I had not thought of him or wondered where he had come to. I wondered now, idly, whether it would be worth the trouble to avenge myself and her.

So I rejoiced that Yarrel had come, and grieved that Yarrel had come bringing Izia, and then simply stopped feeling and *was* while they were there.

And after they had gone, I went to Himaggery, where he sat in his high, mist-filled room and asked him whether he would still accept my help, my Talents and my help, in whatever it was he intended to do. Mertyn was there with him. It was being said that Mertyn would stay, would not return to the Schooltown, so

I thought the matter might well be discussed with them both.

"Ah, you see," said Himaggery to my thalan. "It is precisely as Windlow said." Then, turning to me, "Windlow told me you would come into this very room and say that very thing, Peter. He did not know when it would be. Ah. Ah—but his vision was wrong in one thing. He thought he would be here, too. Tshah. I shall miss him."

"As I will, also," I said. Oh, Windlow, I thought, why did you not simply tell me before I left the Bright Demesne! If you saw the threat, knew the danger, why didn't you tell me. . . . But there was no answer to that. He rested softly in my mind and did not answer though he was present, as he had foreseen.

So I asked the question of Himaggery again, and this time he told me, yes, he would accept my help with great pleasure. It was precisely as I thought, of course. We were to locate the Council. We were to bring the blues to the Bright Demesne. We were to find a way to reunite the body and spirit of ten thousand Gamesmen. We were to pursue Justice, for Windlow had desired that. We were, in short, to do enough things to take a lifetime or two, most of them complicated, some of them dangerous, all of them exciting.

And, I had an agenda of my own. Huld, for example, who had called Necromancer Nine on me, Huld who did not know that he had been right. He had called Necromancer Nine on the young Necromancer, Peter; it was his intention that Peter die, and *that* Peter had died indeed. I did not quite know who the Peter who survived would be, but he would not be Dorn, or Didir, or Trandilar.

So I smiled on Himaggery and offered him my hand. Time alone and the Seers knew what would come next. Highest risk, Necromancer Nine. I was not afraid.

The books of the True Game Series
by Sheri S. Tepper
Available from Ace Fantasy:

KING'S BLOOD FOUR
NECROMANCER NINE

and

WIZARD'S ELEVEN
(coming in February 1984)

Stories
⤙ of ⤚
Swords and Sorcery

Fantasy from Ace
fanciful and fantastic!